Witches Academy

by Kerry Marie Sloan

STARGAZER BOOKS
Philadelphia

STARGAZER
BOOKS

This STARGAZER BOOKS paperback edition October 2019

STARGAZER BOOKS and the STARGAZER BOOKS logo
are trademarks of STARGAZER BOOKS LLC.

For information about special discounts for bulk purchases,
book signings, and talks by the author please contact

Special Events - Stargazer Books
info@stargazerbooks.com
or visit our website
www.stargazerbooks.com

Design by Dan Yager

Manufactured in the United States of America

Library of Congress Control Number: 2019949961

ISBN-13: 978-1-944523-11-4
ISBN-10: 1-944523-11-1

To powerful girls inspired to become
even more powerful women.

CONTENTS

Chapter 1
Exile

Emma shifted uncomfortably in the hard, wooden chair. She picked at a small hole in her grey wool skirt as she waited for Ms. Harfield, the headmistress, to speak.

"You do know why you're here, don't you?" asked Ms. Harfield, breaking the uncomfortable silence that had reigned in the room since Emma's arrival.

"Yes," mumbled Emma, avoiding Ms. Harfield's eyes. Emma had been in this situation many times before, but today was somehow different. There was a gravity to Ms. Harfield's voice that was new.

Emma nervously pushed back her hair, a tangled black mass that always seemed to be falling in her face. She wiped her sweaty palms on her worn skirt before she raised her eyes to Ms. Harfield's face

"Why did you do it, Emma?" asked Ms. Harfield. "There was no need for such a display."

"You don't understand," interrupted Emma, her anger rising. "Miss Snipes is a bully...she..."

"Enough," said Ms. Harfield, holding up her hand to stop Emma in mid-sentence. "I know Miss Snipes isn't always easy to get along with. But if there was something that she did or said, you should have come to me."

"I know," began Emma, "but she..."

"And," interrupted Ms. Harfield, "as for being a bully, I've heard the same thing said about you. You're also known for being quick tempered and unfriendly."

Emma flushed and looked away. She didn't have anything

to say in her own defense. She knew what Ms. Harfield said was true.

"What's my punishment this time?" asked Emma glumly. She wasn't looking forward to the drudgery that was in store for her.

"I don't think you understand the seriousness of the situation," began Ms. Harfield, looking at Emma closely.

"What do you mean?" said Emma.

"I mean that Miss Snipes is the daughter of the head of our Board of Trustees. She's lodged a formal complaint against you with the board for...." Ms. Harfield paused for a moment to refer to one of many pieces of paper she had on the desk before her. "For conduct unbecoming of a student at the Williamson Preparatory School."

Emma's heart sank. She looked down at the ornate carpet that covered the floor of Ms. Harfield's office, nervously tracing the pattern of one of the vines with her foot. She was afraid to look at Ms. Harfield.

"What does that mean?" whispered Emma finally.

"That means that you're going to be expelled from this school," answered Ms. Harfield slowly, pronouncing every word distinctly so that her meaning wouldn't be misunderstood.

"But...." began Emma.

"There are no buts about it," replied Ms. Harfield, sternly. "With your disciplinary record, there's nothing anyone can do or say."

"Where am I supposed to go?" asked Emma, with a slight quaver in her voice.

Ms. Harfield looked at Emma, her gaze softening slightly. "I fought for you Emma...I really did, but the board's decision was unanimous....and final," she said softly.

After a moment's pause, Ms. Harfield cleared her throat and began shuffling through the papers on her desk. "The board has decided to send you to reform school...." she began.

"Oh no!" cried Emma involuntarily, her voice shaking.

"Anywhere but there! I can change...I know I can!"

"Emma," said Ms. Harfield, as gently as she could, "it's not a subject that's up for discussion."

Emma fought as hard as she could against the tears that were gathering in her dark eyes. She had never cried in front of anyone before. She tried to summon back the tough facade with which she normally faced the world, but it was impossible.

A tear escaped from her eye and rolled slowly down her cheek. "Please Ms. Harfield," she whispered. "There has to be a way...this is the only home I've ever known. Don't send me away."

Ms. Harfield continued sorting through the papers on her desk for a few moments before looking up at Emma. She gazed at her for a long time before letting out a sigh.

"Oh Emma," she said finally. "Why do you have to make everything so difficult?"

Emma hung her head. She didn't know how to respond.

"Can I trust you?" asked Ms. Harfield, suddenly.

Emma looked up, startled at the change in Ms. Harfield's tone.

"Trust me with what?" she asked, uncertainly.

Ms. Harfield was looking at her intently.

"If I give you another chance, will you change?" she asked

Emma looked at Ms. Harfield in surprise. She paused for a moment, summoning up all of her strength and determination. "I know I've been awful," she said finally, "but I think I can change. I know there's good in me...there must be. I promise I'll try as hard as I can to be better."

Ms. Harfield nodded slowly and then reached for a set of keys that were on a hook behind her desk. She selected an ornate but rusty key, the largest one on the bunch, and slowly inserted it into a keyhole in one of the drawers in her massive mahogany desk. The drawer screeched and groaned as she pulled it open, as if in protest at being disturbed. After rummaging around in the drawer for a moment, she took out a small, leather bound book and placed it on her desk carefully. A thin layer of dust was visible on the book's worn black cover.

"I have to make a few phone calls before everything is finalized," said Ms. Harfield gravely. "But you don't have to worry about reform school. I'm sending you somewhere else...."

Emma almost sobbed with relief. She felt as if she'd been given a second chance at life.

"I won't let you down," she said.

"Don't let either of us down," replied Ms. Harfield gently.

*****

It was early morning, the day of Emma's departure from the Williamson school. There was a chill in the fall air and a fine mist was falling, making the gray day even gloomier. Emma wiped a few stray rain drops off her face and tried to look brave, but she was having a difficult time. She was leaving the only home she'd ever had. How she was going to fit in anywhere else?

"You're sure you have everything?" asked Miss Johnson sharply, breaking into Emma's mournful train of thought.

Emma winced at her tone. Miss Johnson, a stern, elderly spinster, was one of her least favorite teachers at the school. Why had she been selected to see her off?

"If only Ms. Harfield were here," Emma thought to herself. "All of this would be much easier."

Before replying to Miss Johnson's question, Emma glanced down at her small, slightly battered suitcase. As with most of her possessions, she had inherited the bag from an earlier attendee of the school. A garish floral pattern ran wildly across its front and back. Its burnished wooden handle was slightly askew, constantly threatening to break off in one's hand. Emma detested the suitcase, but it was all she had.

"Yes," replied Emma finally. "That's everything. I don't have much."

"I can see that," snorted Miss Johnson, derisively. As she spoke, she glanced impatiently at her watch.

"Are you sure you know where you're going?" Miss Johnson asked, for at least the third time that morning.

"Yes," said Emma, glancing again at the crumpled piece of paper she held tightly in her hand.

On it, in Ms. Harfield's immaculate script, were concise directions for Emma's journey....first the early morning taxi ride to the bus station, then the long bus trip, and then a second cab ride to her final destination...her new school. Emma's hand strayed towards her coat pocket, where she had carefully stowed the money for the taxi, her bus ticket, and a letter from Ms. Harfield to the director of the new school.

"Ms. Harfield made sure I had everything before she left last night," said Emma.

"Well," snapped Miss Johnson, "I don't know what's keeping the taxi, but it's already ten minutes late. I'm not going to stand out here with you all morning."

Emma sighed and looked away from Miss Johnson's scowling face. Normally she would have gotten angry and replied with a cruel remark of her own. But she was too tired and depressed this morning. Instead, she looked at the large brick mansion behind her, wondering if this would be the last time she ever saw it.

"Finally!" barked Miss Johnson, breaking into Emma's reverie. "The taxi is here!"

Emma looked down the long semi-circular drive that fronted the building. A taxi was slowly making its way towards the entrance of the school where she stood with Miss Johnson.

"Not much of a crowd to see you off," said Miss Johnson, sarcastically.

Emma winced again. She looked wistfully towards the school, still and silent in the early morning light. She knew she wasn't well liked among her classmates, but she had hoped....

"It doesn't matter," said Emma sharply, her dark green eyes

flashing angrily. "I wasn't expecting anyone," she added, shooting a defiant glance at the abrasive woman.

Despite her sadness, Emma wasn't going to let Miss Johnson get the better of her on her last day at Williamson.

Suddenly, a small figure darted from the front door of the school. She ran towards Emma as fast as she could, and, when she reached her, threw her arms around her and sobbed.

"I didn't think I'd make it in time," the girl said, as she looked up into Emma's face.

"Lindsay!" said Miss Johnson angrily. "What are you doing out here at this hour?"

The short, slightly plump little girl ignored Miss Johnson's question. "We wanted you to have this," said the girl, as she shoved something warm and metal into Emma's hand. "It's from all of us."

Emma looked at Lindsay for a moment, and then looked at the object in her hand. It was a small silver chain with a crescent moon hanging from it.

Emma tried to say something, but found she couldn't form the words. There was a lump in her throat and tears threatened to spill out of her eyes. "Thank you," she finally whispered.

Lindsay hugged her one more time, stuck her tongue out at Miss Johnson and then darted back into the building.

"Would you just get in the cab so I can go back to bed?" Miss Johnson snarled.

Emma merely nodded and headed towards the cab. She wasn't going to cry, especially not in front of Miss Johnson. She climbed in quickly, keeping her face averted from Miss Johnson's angry scowl.

"Good bye Williamson," Emma whispered, as she took one last look at the school from the cab window.

*****

The day had been very long for Emma. The weather hadn't improved much, and, now that it was evening, the mist of the

6

morning had turned into a steady, cold drizzle. Every so often there was a rumbling of thunder in the distance.

Emma had fallen asleep on the bus ride, and had almost missed her destination. She had been awoken by the bus driver shouting at her, and she now felt groggy and grumpy.

Thankfully, she was almost at her journey's end. The cab driver had just turned down the street where the school was located. Emma was grateful. She didn't think she could take any more traveling today.

"You sure this is where you want to go?" asked the cab driver, doubtfully, as he maneuvered the cab down the dark, narrow street. There were few houses and no street lights.

Emma rechecked the directions Ms. Harfield had given to her. "1122 Blackwood Street," she said. "That's the address."

"Alight," he replied skeptically. "But I wouldn't want to be left out here by myself in the middle of the night."

Emma looked out the window and shivered. She tried to ignore the cab driver's words, but he was right. It was creepy out here.

"I'll be fine," she snapped, trying not to let her fear show.

A moment later, the cab stopped and the driver peered out the window.

"Here we are," he said, as he looked at a battered mailbox that stood near the side of the road.

"1122 Blackwood Street," he read, looking at the address etched into the side of the mailbox. "I guess this is the right place."

A long driveway extended from the road and disappeared into the dark woods that lined both sides of the street. Emma could only hope that the school lay at the end of the driveway. She couldn't see anything through the thick trees.

Emma looked at the driveway and shuddered. This was not what she had expected. However, she had no choice. She paid the cab driver, gathered her things, and slowly got out of the cab.

"You sure you don't want me to wait?" he asked, looking a

bit concerned as Emma began to make her way towards the forbidding driveway.

"I'll be fine," she said again, more sharply than she had intended. She knew the cab driver was trying to be nice, but she didn't want him to see how afraid she really was.

"Okay," he said in resignation. "Suit yourself."

Emma stood still for a moment, watching the lights from the cab disappear down the road. Soon she was left alone in the gloom.

Emma was frightened, but she knew she had no choice but to walk down the driveway. She took a deep breath, gathered up what little courage she had left, and began picking her way carefully down the gravel covered drive. As she walked, the wet gravel slipped under her feet, making it hard for her to keep her balance. After a few moments, Emma's pace slowed even more. The driveway was rutted and uneven and it was difficult to find a safe path. Clearly this was not a roadway that was used very often. The trees were thick overhead and their dark limbs dipped low over the drive, as if they were trying to reach out and touch her.

Suddenly a loud noise rent the evening air. Emma almost screamed and then, before she knew it, she lost her footing and fell to her knees. Some sort of a creature screeched again and flew past her face, its wings almost brushing her cheek. She looked up quickly and made out the shape of an owl, winging its way towards the trees.

For a moment she felt a sense of relief...it was only an owl, not a bat, as she had first feared. But her relief was short lived. She still wasn't at the end of the driveway. Who knew what other horrible creatures might be lying in wait for her?

After what seemed like an eternity of walking, Emma finally saw a faint light ahead. She could dimly make out the outline of a massive stone building looming out of the twilight. She shuddered again, the foreboding sight did not make her feel any better.

Emma swallowed her fear and picked her way carefully

down an uneven stone path that led to the entrance of the building. She knocked loudly, using the large, rusty iron knocker that adorned the huge front door. As Emma watched, the door swung open, as if of its own accord.

There was a moment of blackness, and then a light leaped out of the darkness. A candle, held by a gnarled hand loomed into sight. Emma could dimly make out the shapes of two old women, one holding the candle and one standing in the background.

She wanted to scream, but no sound would come.

"Welcome to Witches' Academy," said one of the women, in a low, creaky voice.

Before Emma knew it, she was pulled into the building and the door slammed shut behind her.

Chapter 2
The Academy

Emma's eyes slowly fluttered open. For a moment, she didn't know where she was. This wasn't her dorm room at Williamson. Where was she? She was lying on a large couch and her head was propped up on a thick, fluffy pillow. The couch was upholstered in an incredibly, soft velvety fabric. She turned her head and saw a bright, richly decorated room, dark mahogany paneled walls, a thick, plush rug, substantial upholstered chairs, an ornately carved hearth, and a roaring fire.

Emma started to sit up, trying to remember where she was and what had happened.

As she did so, she noticed two elderly women who were hovering anxiously over her.

"Oh! What a relief!" said one of the women. "We didn't know if we'd scared the life out of you!"

"We were beginning to think you'd never wake up," said the other woman.

As she looked up at the two women, Emma's memory returned...the long journey from Williamson, the harrowing walk up the driveway, and the horrifying moment of entering the school. She must have fainted from fear. But surely this couldn't be the same place...and these couldn't be the same women....

"Am I at..." began Emma, uncertainly.

"Yes," answered one of the women, "you made it to your new school and new home. We know you're Emma Yeats. We have your letter from Ms. Harfield."

"Are either of you Ms. Stanwick?" asked Emma, looking doubtfully from one to the other. "Ms. Harfield said I was supposed to ask for her."

"Oh goodness no!" laughed one of the women. "She's rarely ever here. But we take care of the place for her. And we'll take good care of you."

"But where are our manners?!" said the other woman. "We haven't even introduced ourselves."

Emma was sitting upright on the couch by now and she gazed curiously at the two women before her. They looked almost identical. Both were short and stout, both had round, rosy faces, and both had long white hair. They were both dressed completely in gray. The only difference Emma could see was that one of the women, who was just a bit shorter than the other, had her hair in an elaborate bun. The other woman wore her hair in a long braid down her back.

"I'm Thora Goodleigh," said the slightly shorter woman with the bun.

"And I'm Nedra Goodleigh," said the woman with the braid.

"We're sisters," Thora added, by way of explanation.

Emma smiled slightly at Thora's explanation... as if she hadn't noticed the resemblance.

"We're sorry we gave you such a fright when you came in," Nedra said. "We had some horrible thunderstorms earlier this evening and the power was out. That's why we had candles when you arrived. As you can see, it's normally much brighter in here."

"You dropped your letter when you came in," she continued. "We hope you don't mind that we picked it up..." she added, holding out the letter that Emma had brought with her from Ms. Harfield.

"No," said Emma. "It's for you...or at least for whoever is in charge."

"Ms. Harfield is an old friend of ours, and of everyone here. She recommends you very highly," said Nedra, looking at the letter.

"It seems that you had a bit of trouble at Williamson," added Thora.

Emma reddened. She could feel her defenses rising. But, instead of snapping out an angry retort, she turned away and looked at the fire. She didn't want to break her promise to Ms. Harfield.

She took a few deep breaths and then said, in a small, low voice, "I was kicked out."

"Yes," said Thora, understandingly. "We know. But we also know that you're very talented. Ms. Harfield says you were the top student in your class. We know that you'll do well here."

Emma looked at Thora uncertainly. She was surprised at how kind both of these strangers were being to her. What did they want?

"Thank you," she said slowly. "I'm going to try to do my best."

"Of course you are," said Nedra. "And we'll do everything we can to help you."

"Now," said Thora, "you must be starving! I'm sure you haven't eaten anything since this morning. We're already well past the dinner hour, but we ordered some sandwiches from the kitchen for you. Is that okay?"

Emma nodded. Until Thora had mentioned food she hadn't realized how hungry she was.

"And, in the meantime," began Nedra, "we can get you acclimated to your new home."

Suddenly something tugged at the corner of Emma's mind. "When I first came in...before I fainted..." began Emma. "I think one of you said something about witc..."

Before Emma could finish her sentence, Thora cut her off. "Ms. Harfield didn't tell you much about the school, did she?"

Emma paused for a moment. "No, not really," she said. "Nothing specific. I just assumed she was sending me to another school like Williamson."

Thora and Nedra exchanged a meaningful glance.

Thora nodded and then looked towards Emma again. "Well, perhaps it's better that we save some things for tomorrow. We don't want to overwhelm you on the first day."

Emma looked at the two women curiously. Clearly there was something that they weren't telling her. But, rather than continue her questions, Emma decided to wait. There were other things that she was curious about.

"The school is so hidden away," said Emma. "I wasn't sure I was in the right place at first. It looks almost abandoned from the street."

"You're right about that," said Thora. "We're so sorry we weren't outside to greet you and walk you up the driveway when you arrived. It's not the easiest walk to do on one's own in the dark. That driveway certainly has seen better days."

"But that's the way Ms. Stanwick likes it," explained Nedra. "She prefers to keep the school somewhat of a secret. It's always been that way, for as long as I can remember."

"But why?" asked Emma.

"Oh lots of reasons," said Thora, vaguely. "You'll understand more as you're here longer."

"It looks so different inside," said Emma, looking around at the opulent room. "I thought Williamson was nice, but this is incredible. Is the whole school like this?"

"Oh yes!" said Nedra, enthusiastically. "We have the best of everything for everyone. You're going to enjoy living here."

"I suppose the girls who come here are well off? Just like the girls at Williamson?" asked Emma, starting to feel her spirits sink. She had been hoping for a fresh start. She didn't want a repeat of her experience at Williamson.

"There's no lack of resources at our school," said Thora, slowly. "But our girls come from all sorts of different backgrounds....not all of them are wealthy."

"Our girls are not snobs," said Nedra, bluntly, "if that's what you're asking. "We teach everyone here to be kind. I think you'll see that fairly quickly."

After a moment, Emma began speaking again, in a small,

nervous voice that was nothing like her normal speaking voice. "Do you really think people can learn to be kind?"

"Of course dear," said Thora, looking at her closely. "Everyone has the capacity to be kind."

"Even people who don't know how?" said Emma, in a voice that was barely audible.

Nedra walked over to Emma and put a reassuring hand on the girl's shoulder. "Yes," she answered, in a strong firm voice. "We'll show you that it's possible."

"And now," said Thora, "we're going to see what's keeping those sandwiches. They should have been here already! We'll be back in a moment."

As soon as the two women were gone and Emma was alone, tiredness overwhelmed her. She'd had such a long day. And she was feeling so worn out and alone. Emma was surprised at herself and her own emotions. She must be exhausted or she wouldn't have opened up to Thora and Nedra in the way that she had. Normally she kept her feelings to herself.

Perhaps she would just close her eyes for a minute or two. She'd be awake before Thora and Nedra came back. But, in just a few moments, Emma was sound asleep.

*****

Emma awoke again on the couch in the study. Light streaming in the front window caused her to stir and then to open her eyes. As she woke, she noticed a large gray cat curled up at her feet. Emma recoiled instinctively. She hated cats, but for some reason they loved her. This cat was no exception. She blinked her eyes at Emma a few times, and then settled back down on the couch.

Emma wrinkled her noise and pushed the cat off the couch with her foot as she sat up. As she was disengaging herself from the cat, Thora walked into the room. She was carrying a large plate with what looked like breakfast food.

Emma reddened slightly. She hoped that Thora hadn't seen her kick the cat. What a way to start off at her new school!

"I see you've met Samantha," said Thora, with a dark look at the cat.

"Sorry," mumbled Emma, apologetically. "I don't really like cats."

Thora gave her an approving look. "None of us do," she said. "Unfortunately they tend to like us."

She paused for a moment and glanced at the retreating cat, who was gazing mournfully at Emma. "And it seems that Samantha especially likes you. She doesn't usually take to the new girls so quickly."

"I've brought you some breakfast," continued Thora. "It's all I could scrounge up this morning. We didn't want to wake you, so you missed the normal breakfast meal. I hope this is enough."

Emma glanced at the huge plate of food. It looked like enough for about five people.

"I'm sorry I fell asleep last night," she said, as she took the plate from Thora. "I think I was exhausted from traveling. And thank you for breakfast....Thora?" she said, a bit uncertainly. The woman had her hair done up in another elaborate bun, not a braid like Nedra. Emma hoped that she hadn't changed her hair style from the previous evening.

"Yes, it's Thora," laughed the woman. "I don't know why everyone has so much trouble telling me and my sister apart. I don't think we look anything alike."

Emma smiled and began eating with relish. She was starving after missing dinner the previous day.

Emma looked around the room curiously as she ate. The school seemed so beautiful and peaceful. And Thora and Nedra were so nice. Perhaps she would like it here. Maybe she had finally found a home.

Thora looked at Emma and smiled. "We do have a few things to talk about before we start getting you oriented to the school."

16

Emma nodded her head, as she finished her first piece of toast. This food was better than anything she'd ever had at Williamson.

Emma smiled and said, "Last night I was so exhausted I think I must have been imagining things. I thought you said something about witches when I first came in. That seems crazy now!"

Thora came over to Emma and sat down next to her gently on the couch.

"Actually...."said Thora slowly, "We did say witches. The school that you are at is called Witches' Academy."

Emma dropped the piece of toast that she had just picked up. "What?" she said, incredulously.

"We teach girls how to be witches here. I wish Ms. Harfield had prepared you a little bit more, but perhaps it's better this way."

Emma was speechless. What was Thora trying to say? Was she crazy?

"I'm sure it will take you awhile to get used to the idea," said Thora gently.

Emma pushed her half eaten breakfast away, her appetite now gone.

Thora looked at her with concern. "Would you like me to tell you a little more about the school?" she asked kindly.

Emma nodded her head reluctantly. She didn't know what else to do. She felt as if her world had been turned upside down.

"And perhaps I can brush your hair while we're talking?" suggested Thora.

Emma reddened slightly and her hand went up to her hair. As usual, it was a tangled mess.

"I must look a fright," she said, starting to fumble with her hair and trying to straighten her wrinkled, travel-stained clothes.

"No," said Thora. "You look like a girl who's been traveling for a long time."

Emma's embarrassment melted away under Thora's kind gaze. Normally, she would have been angry at any mention of her appearance. But Thora, crazy or not, was somehow different.

"I never let other people brush my hair," said Emma, still a bit wary. "It never stays untangled. It's always a mess, no matter what I do."

"Well," said Thora, gesturing towards her magnificent hairdo, "I do have a bit of experience with hair. We'll see how I do with yours. And I promise I won't hurt you."

Emma was doubtful. It was painful enough trying to get the tangles out of her hair herself. Letting someone else do it didn't seem like a good idea.

Thora sat down next to Emma and retrieved a small, golden brush and comb from a delicate beaded purse which she was carrying.

"Now," she said, as she began straightening Emma's hair. "You relax and listen and I'll tell you about Witches' Academy. And if you have any questions you can stop me and I'll try to answer you as best I can."

Emma nodded uncertainly and turned around. It didn't seem like she had much of a choice. She readied herself for a crazy story from Thora and for the discomfort of Thora's brushing and combing, but to her surprise, she didn't feel anything unpleasant. Thora was gently pulling the golden comb through her hair, but instead of getting snarled in tangles, the comb was going smoothly and evenly.

"Witches' Academy," said Thora, "has been around in one form or another for many, many years. We've been in this location for at least 100 years, or perhaps just a bit less. I tend to lose count. The purpose of the school is to train young girls to be witches."

"But that's impossible!" protested Emma.

Thora sighed at Emma's reaction. "Unfortunately, just like you, people don't really believe in witches anymore. We used to have more girls applying to the school than we could accept. Now there are only about 30 or so in the entire school. And the numbers keep falling every year. There just doesn't seem to be much demand for witches in the outside world anymore..."

Thora paused and sighed again. "But that's another story. For now, all you need to know is that you're going to learn to be a witch, among other things. We do teach all of the normal subjects as well. But the primary focus is on witchcraft."

Thora paused for a moment, put down her comb, and picked up the golden brush. "Your hair is coming out wonderfully," she said, happily. "You have such beautiful hair too. It's a pleasure to help you with it. I'm not hurting you, am I?"

"No," said Emma, in surprise. She had almost forgotten Thora was combing her hair. Despite herself, she was caught up in Thora's story. Of course, she knew it was all nonsense, it had to be! But Thora made it all sound so interesting.

Thora raised the brush and began pulling it softly through Emma's hair. "Now..." she said, "where was I?"

"Ah yes, what you're going to learn here. Ms. Harfield indicated in her letter that you had just started in the high school at Williamson...so that would make you about thirteen or fourteen?"

"I'm thirteen," said Emma.

"Yes, perfect," said Thora. "We do have a few girls your age. And you can take the normal classes with them. As for the witchcraft part of your education...I think we'll have to put you in with the younger girls. We start with 7 year olds...I hope you don't mind..."

Emma didn't know how to respond. She couldn't believe what Thora was telling her. It was all so crazy!

"Whatever you want me to do is fine," she mumbled.

"I knew you wouldn't have a problem with it," said Thora, smilingly. "And I do think you'll learn quickly. Not everyone has an aptitude for it...most of our girls come from families with generations of witches. That seems to help. But I think

Ms. Harfield was right about you...there's something there...I can feel it too..."

Emma almost laughed out loud. What was Thora talking about? Witches weren't real!

Suddenly a thought occurred to Emma. "How did Ms. Harfield know about Witches' Academy?" she asked.

Thora looked amused. "Ms. Harfield is a witch too," she said. "Not currently practicing of course. With the lack of demand for witches it's hard for any of us to find jobs that use all of our unique skills. But Ms. Harfield was one of our more gifted pupils. It's unfortunate that she's had to lower herself to being a headmistress of a school...but there are lots like her...all wonderfully talented women..."

"Are there lots of witches out in the world doing other things?" asked Emma, unbelievingly.

"Oh yes!" said Thora. "More than I can count! Most in very important jobs...heads of companies and presidents of corporations, government officials, judges, doctors, and lawyers...you name the profession and we've got someone there. Of course, some of our more specialized witches go on to other careers more suited for their training, but you'll learn all about that in good time..."

"But now," said Thora, "you have to look at your hair....it looks absolutely stunning!"

Thora pulled a small golden mirror from her bag and handed it to Emma. Emma slowly held the mirror up to her face and took a tentative look. She wasn't sure she would like what she saw.

Emma gasped as she looked. Her hair, which was always a tangled mess, was smooth and straight. It fell gently down her back in soft waves, with not a tangle in sight.

"How did you do that?" said Emma, shocked.

"I have my tricks," answered Thora, with a smile. "I am a witch you know."

Thora stood back and looked at Emma, appraisingly. "You look quite lovely really," she said. "Such beautiful dark hair and you have such interesting green eyes...more hazel than green really..."

Emma blushed. She wasn't used to anyone taking an interest in her personal appearance.

"You are a bit pale," said Thora, with a note of concern. "And a bit too skinny I think...but that'll change here. We'll get you out in the sun, and once you start eating the meals our cook makes you'll be the picture of health. They didn't take the best care of you at Williamson, did they?"

Emma didn't know what to say. Nobody had cared about her at Williamson. Nobody had ever cared for her anywhere.

She was saved the embarrassment by a tentative knock at the door.

Chapter 3
The Academy (Part 2)

"Oh!" said Thora, at the sound of the knocking on the door. "That must be Cora. I'd almost forgotten we'd asked her to come meet you this morning. She's one of the girls that I mentioned who's about your age. She'll be showing you around the school today and getting you oriented."

"Come in Cora," said Thora, as she walked briskly over to the study door.

Thora ushered in a young girl who looked to be about the same age as Emma. However, that was where the similarities ended. Where Emma was all tangles and angles, Cora was delicate and lovely. Softly curling blond hair, sparkling blue eyes, and a perfect pink and white complexion...she was the exact opposite of Emma.

Emma's heart sank. She had been hoping for a possible friend. Instead, this girl looked just like all of the girls at Williamson...pretty and perfect.

After greeting Thora, Cora walked across the room to where Emma was sitting. Emma braced herself. She already knew she wasn't going to get along with the perfect Cora.

But, to Emma's surprise, Cora's face broke into a radiant smile as soon as she reached Emma's side. She stretched out her hand and said, "I'm Cora...and you must be Emma. We've been expecting you. We've all been so excited since we heard you were coming. It's not often that we get a new girl here!"

Emma was taken aback. For a moment, she didn't respond. And then, finally, she stretched out her hand to Cora. She smiled cautiously and said, "It's nice to meet you."

She couldn't think of anything else to say. There had to be a catch. Maybe Cora was just being nice because Thora was in the room with them.

"Cora, I want you to show Emma everything," said Thora. "Give her the grand tour. Then you can eat lunch, get her set up in the dormitory, and maybe bring her to one of your classes if you have time. Does that sound good to you?"

"Perfect," said Cora happily. She smiled at Emma again, grabbed her by the hand, and pulled her up off the couch. "We're going to have a wonderful day together," she said, as she led Emma to the door.

"I'll see you two at dinner," said Thora. "And be careful in the library....you know how it can get in there!"

"Of course," said Cora. "We'll be careful."

Before Emma could even pause for breath, they were out in the hallway, Cora leading her swiftly down the corridor. Emma glanced around her as they went. A jumble of dark wooden wainscoting, elaborate carvings, and ancient oil paintings met her eyes.

"I'm so excited!" said Cora. "I have so much to show you and we have so much to talk about! I don't even know where to begin..."

"Um, Cora," interrupted Emma. "Could you answer one question before we get started?"

"Sure," said Cora. "Whatever you want to know..."

"Thora and Nedra seem like very nice old women, but are they really in charge here?"

"Of course," said Cora. "At least most of the time. The real head of the school is Ms. Stanwick, but she's only here every so often. Thora and Nedra keep things going while she's gone."

Emma paused for a moment and then said, "I don't really know how to put this...but...are they crazy?"

Cora looked at her curiously. "Whatever would give you that idea?"

"They told me a long story about witches...and they said this school was called Witches' Academy...but of course, that's not possible!"

Cora took a deep breath and then began to laugh. "I forgot," she said. "All of this is new to you...you're not from one of the families..."

Emma looked at her for a moment and then said, "You seem pretty normal to me....definitely not crazy. You don't really believe all of this stuff about witches, do you? I mean, this looks like a pretty normal school ..."

Cora patted Emma on the arm, and then looked at her seriously. "I know you've been through a lot. How about I give you the tour of the school and then, once you've seen a bit more, I can answer your questions."

Emma sighed and shrugged her shoulders. "Okay," she said, doubtfully.

As she followed Cora, she thought to herself, "What have I gotten myself into? Everyone here is crazy...."

"Let's get you set up in the dorm first," said Cora over her shoulder. "We can get you a uniform there too. After that, I'll show you around the rest of the school, and by then it should be lunchtime."

"Sure," said Emma, following after her.

Cora led her up the ornate main staircase in the large entryway and then turned sharply to the right.

"Here we are," Cora said, as she led Emma through a set of double doors into a very long, bright, high-ceilinged room

Emma gasped as she entered the dorm. The room was huge! It was partitioned into small rooms, each furnished with beautiful furniture....soft, comfortable beds, large wooden dressers, plush carpets...it was unbelievable!

"This is nothing like Williamson," said Emma, incredulously. "Everything is so nice! Are these rooms for everyone, or just the wealthy students? And it's huge! There must be room for at least fifty girls in here.

Cora laughed at all of Emma's questions. "Yes, these rooms are for all of the girls...no special treatment here. And yes, there is room for at least fifty girls...but most of the rooms are

25

empty. The academy isn't what it used to be."

"But here," said Cora, a little more brightly. "This is your room! It's going to be perfect for you. It's right next to mine, so, if we position your bed against this wall, we can talk before we go to bed at night. I know we're going to be great friends!"

Emma looked at her doubtfully, still wary. She never had any real friends before, especially not girls her own age. And not girls who looked like Cora.

"Sure," said Emma. "It looks nice, probably the nicest room I've ever had!"

Emma smiled a little as she surveyed her new room. Maybe it wouldn't be so bad living here, if she could just find a few people who weren't crazy. She sat down on the bed and sunk into the fluffy mattress.

"This bed is heavenly!" said Emma.

"Everything here is heavenly," laughed Cora.

"Are those for me?" asked Emma, suddenly noticing a huge vase of flowers on the dresser.

Cora nodded, "They're your welcome flowers," she said with a smile.

Then she looked over at the flowers and frowned. "But they're not looking their best, are they?"

"What do you mean?" asked Emma. This was her first time receiving flowers. To her, they looked fine.

Cora walked over to the flowers and touched a few of the blossoms. In a moment, the flowers had become exquisitely beautiful, glowing and sparkling with health and vitality.

"What did you do to them?" asked Emma, incredulously.

"Nothing really," said Cora with a shrug. "But let's not get distracted by flowers. We have the very important matter of clothes to deal with right now."

Cora looked closely at Emma, as if sizing her up.

"I did bring a few things with me," said Emma hesitantly. She looked around, almost expecting to see her dreaded suitcase somewhere in the room.

"We can have someone bring your bag up later. I'm sure

Nedra or Thora has it somewhere," replied Cora. "But for now, let's find you a uniform, and maybe a few other things..."

Cora led Emma over to the opposite side of the room where a very large, very long closet dominated the wall. "This is what we call our communal closet," smiled Cora. "It's sort of a place for us to go shopping."

Cora slid open several of the doors and Emma gasped. She had expected to see a bunch of well-worn uniforms and perhaps a few "hand-me-down" dresses. But everything in the closet looked brand new! And it wasn't just filled with uniforms. There were also beautiful dresses, skirts, and tops in just about every color and material that Emma could imagine.

"Nice, isn't it?" said Cora.

"But is all of this stuff for the students here?" asked Emma, unbelievingly.

"Of course," answered Cora. "Who else would it be for?" "Now," she said, "you definitely need a few uniforms, so let's take these. New shoes, of course....I think these will do nicely," said Cora, sweeping up a pair from the floor of the closet. "And then, if you'd like some new clothes, just grab a few outfits. We'll put them in your room when we're done."

Emma looked flabbergasted. She hesitated, staring at the clothes in front of her, as if unsure what to do.

"Is anything wrong?" asked Cora. "If you don't see anything you like, we can look down at the other end of the closet...it's really filled with anything you can imagine..."

"No," said Emma, haltingly. "It's not that. Everything is beautiful! It's just that I've never picked any of my own clothes before. I don't really know what to do."

Cora looked at her new friend with kind eyes. "It's okay," said Cora. "Maybe we can start slow. Just take one or two things for now. Whatever you like....I can help if you want."

Emma hesitantly reached out and took a navy blue skirt and a white sweater.

"I think those would look lovely on you!" said Cora, encouragingly. "And how about a dress? I can see you in purple or maybe burgundy."

"What about this one?" asked Emma, uncertainly, pointing at a deep purple, silky dress.

"Perfect!" said Cora. "I was going to pick that one for you too!"

Cora gathered up all of Emma's new things and toted them over to Emma's room, Emma following meekly in tow.

"Let's get these things put away and then we'll start our tour," said Cora, happily, clearly pleased with all of Emma's new acquisitions. "Maybe you should change too. I think you'll like the uniforms here. They're really nice."

Emma nodded slowly. She'd be glad to be rid of her old clothes. It would feel as if she was making a fresh start.

Suddenly a thought occurred to Emma. "But is anything going to fit?" she asked. "We didn't even look at the sizes!"

Cora laughed. "I don't think you need to worry about that....anything that comes out of that closet tends to fit the wearer. But....just in case..." Cora held her hand over the pile of new clothes that she had placed on Emma's bed and mumbled something unintelligible. "That should do it," she smiled.

"You get changed," she said, as she walked back towards the wardrobe. "I have one more thing to get for you!"

Emma looked at Cora's retreating back and sighed in dismay. She seemed so kind and normal. But it was obvious that she had just pretended to cast a spell on Emma's new clothes! Cora had to be just as crazy as Nedra and Thora. It seemed so nice at this school. Emma hated to think that she'd have to leave or run away. But she couldn't live in a place where everyone was crazy!

Emma began changing, trying to push the thought of witches out of her head. It felt good to take off her old Williamson clothes, even if she was only putting on a uniform. She slipped on the white shirt that Cora had given her. It fit well, but that wasn't a surprise. Shirts were easy to fit. The skirt and blazer were a different matter. Emma doubted they would fit correctly, despite Cora's assurances. The skirt was very nice...gray wool, A-line...Emma slipped it on slowly. As she slid the skirt onto her waist, she felt something just a bit strange. She couldn't say for certain, but it almost felt as if the skirt shrunk just a little bit. Emma adjusted the skirt. It fit perfectly, almost as if it was made for her. She must be imagining things! All of this talk of witches was getting to her head. She began putting the blazer on...also lovely...navy blue with a gray insignia on one side. As she did so, she felt the same queer sensation that had accompanied the skirt. The blazer felt a tad small as she slipped it on, but, as she adjusted it, it seemed to grow just a bit bigger, again, fitting her perfectly.

"This isn't possible!" said Emma, shaking herself. "I'm just imagining things!"

She bent down to take off her socks and shoes. Emma hoped the shoes wouldn't fit. It would make her feel a bit less crazy.

She slid on the socks that Cora had given her with the shoes, lovely gray woven knee socks, softer than anything she had ever felt before.

"And now for the shoes," she mumbled to herself.

Emma tentatively slid one of her feet into the gray oxford shoes that Cora had picked for her. They were also beautiful, much nicer than anything Emma had ever owned before. As she settled her foot into the shoe, she could almost see the shoe getting just a tiny bit smaller, shrinking to fit her foot. And of course, when she tied the shoe it was a perfect fit. This couldn't be happening? What was going on? Was she crazy too?

Emma rubbed her eyes, and gazed at the shoe on her foot. "I'm imagining things," she said to herself, determinedly. "It was just a coincidence that all of these things fit me."

Despite these assurances, Emma squeezed her eyes tightly shut as she put on the second shoe. She tried to ignore the odd feeling she had of the shoe conforming to her foot.

Just as she finished with the shoes, Cora returned from her errand, holding a long white sash in her hand.

"You look wonderful!" said Cora, as she saw Emma in her new uniform. "Everything fits perfectly, just as I said!"

Cora led Emma over to a long mirror hanging on the wall of her room.

"Look!" she said, indicating Emma's reflection. "Don't you think you look like the perfect academy girl?"

Emma smiled in spite of herself. Despite the oddness that accompanied her new clothes, she was happy with her reflection. Her hair still looked lovely, thanks to Nedra's administrations. And the clothes did look very becoming on her.

"You just need this," said Cora, tying the white sash around her waist. "See, I have one too," said Cora, indicating an identical white sash. "I'll explain more about these later. But all of the girls have one. There are different colors that mean different things."

"What does white mean?" asked Emma, curiously.

"It means undecided," said Cora, blushing slightly. "I'll let you know more about all of that after our tour. But for now, let's get started. You really need to see the academy! It's an incredible old building."

*****

A few moments later Cora and Emma were standing in the academy's magnificent entryway. Directly behind them were the large double doors through which Emma had made her dramatic entrance the previous evening. Before them, was the imposing staircase which led to the dorms and other rooms on the second and third floors. And, to the right and left, were hallways leading to the east and west wings of the school.

Emma gazed around in awe. She had thought Williamson was a nice place. But it was shabby compared to her new home.

"This is incredible!" she said, half to herself, as she admired her surroundings.

30

The entryway was large and open, and, as with the rest of the school, was elegant and luxurious, without being ostentatious. Ornately carved wooden moldings, elaborate inlaid stone floors, stained glass windows, and ancient tapestries adorned the walls, giving the place a magnificent and prosperous feel.

Isn't it beautiful?" said Cora, in agreement. "I sort of take it for granted since I see it all the time. You get used to being surrounded by splendor once you're here for a while."

"I thought this was a good place to start our tour though," continued Cora, "since so much of the school's history is on display here. If you take a look at some of these paintings, you'll see they tell the story of the school's founding and they also depict some of the more famous women who have headed the academy."

Cora was gesturing towards the artifacts and paintings that covered the walls of the entryway. Emma did her best to follow what Cora was saying about the history of the school, but she couldn't keep her mind focused. She couldn't stop thinking about what had just happened upstairs. How had all of the clothes fit her perfectly? And the shoes? There had to be something strange going on, right? But then again, maybe it was just a coincidence. Cora could have chosen clothes that looked like they would fit her. And perhaps she had just imagined the clothes conforming to her body. She hadn't gotten much sleep lately. She had to be overtired. That was the only explanation.

Feeling a bit comforted, Emma dragged her attention back to Cora. She was pointing towards a group of paintings on the wall that showed what looked like the construction of the academy, overseen by a group of fearsome looking women.

"These paintings tell the story of the school's original founders, as you can see," said Cora.

Emma looked a bit more closely at the paintings. She wasn't particularly interested in the history of the academy, but she didn't want Cora to think she was being rude by not paying attention. As she looked, to her astonishment, the figures in the paintings appeared to move. The women, who had looked so fearsome a moment before, seemed to be smiling at her. And, even more incredible, the half-finished building in the painting before her began to take shape and construct itself into the finished academy.

Emma gasped. What was going on? She rubbed her eyes and looked at the painting again. This time, it appeared as she had first seen it. Was Cora trying to trick her?

Cora looked at Emma's bewildered face and laughed. "As I said, the paintings in this hallway tell the history of the school, quite literally, as you can see. You do have to be careful though. Sometimes they aren't completely accurate with all of their facts. They can embellish a bit, make things a bit more dramatic than they actually were...."

Emma was again at a loss for words. She had just about convinced herself that she had imagined the strange events with her clothes. But how to explain the paintings? Was she losing her mind?

Cora looked at Emma and smiled understandingly, "I'm sure all of this is a bit overwhelming for you. That's probably enough history for today anyway. Why don't we continue our tour? I still have a lot to show you."

She took Emma's arm and led her to the right side of the entryway, towards the west wing of the building.

"You've already seen the study," said Cora, gesturing behind her, towards the east wing. "The east wing is the teacher's wing of the academy. Lots of offices and things like that. Students aren't usually allowed down there except for special occasions."

"Back past the stairs is the dining room and kitchen, and a few other rooms...there's a ball room, that's really beautiful. We'll get to that at the end, after we eat lunch."

"But this way," said Cora, continuing towards the right, "is where you'll be spending the most time. All of the classrooms and the library are down here."

Despite the chaos in Emma's mind, she couldn't help being mesmerized by what she saw. The building was truly incredible! As Cora led her down the hallway, she peeped into immaculately clean classrooms, mostly empty, but filled with well stocked bookcases and beautifully carved wooden desks.

At the end of the hallway, was a massive double door, richly carved with a wondrous assortment of fantastical figures. Emma was enchanted.

"And this," said Cora, impressively, "is the library. It's really incredible. The collection is amazing! But, a word of caution, you do need to be careful. I wouldn't recommend coming here alone, and never after dark."

"Why?" said Emma. "Is it haunted or something?"

"Sort of," said Cora, as she cautiously opened one of the doors a crack. Emma was just able to glimpse a bit of the remarkable interior....floor to ceiling bookcases filled with countless rows of books, large tables surrounded by heavy wooden chairs, a massive brick fireplace...before a disturbing whooshing sound caused Cora to abruptly slam the door shut.

"He's not in a good mood today," Cora said, looking a little flustered. "Now may not be the best time to tour the library. I'll be sure to have Nedra or Thora show you around later."

Emma looked at Cora curiously but didn't say anything. What was there to say? Everything about this place was so odd.

"That would be a nice. It looks like a beautiful room...and so many books," she added wistfully.

"Do you like to read?" asked Cora.

"Yes, of course," said Emma. "But I didn't get to read much at Williamson. The library was a bit limited....and I didn't have a lot of free time...."

"Well," said Cora, patting her arm reassuringly. "You'll have lots of time here. And just about any book you'd ever want to read is in that library, trust me."

Emma looked back at the strange room, wondering what could possibly have accounted for Cora's strange behavior.

But, before she could continue her train of thought, she was startled by a loud crashing sound, followed by a bright flash. Emma looked around and saw a closed door that she hadn't noticed before. Cora hadn't mentioned it on her tour.

"What's going on?" said Emma, a bit frightened.

"Oh, that's nothing," said Cora, unconcernedly. "That door leads to the basement...there are a bunch of practice rooms down there.....at least that's what we call them. I'd show you now, but it's a bad time. Esmerelda's down there."

"Who's Esmerelda?" asked Emma.

"She's the oldest girl here...taking her third level exams....but by the sound of it, she's not going to pass again. She's not that good," added Cora in a whisper.

Cora's words were followed by another crashing sound, a thud, and then an incredibly bright flash.

"You'll meet her later," said Cora. "She's very nice, but not gray material, at least not yet She needs a lot more practice."

"Gray material? What does that mean?" asked Emma.

"Oh!" said Cora. "I keep forgetting, you don't know. I'll explain later. But, right now, we have to get to lunch. Today's going to be special. We don't want to be late!"

Emma suddenly realized how hungry she was. This place seemed to have a strange effect on her. She had never really enjoyed eating at Williamson. But now, it seemed that she was hungry all of the time. And everything she had eaten at the school had been so good! How could she not want to eat?

"Sounds good to me!" said Emma, returning Cora's smile shyly.

*****

A few moments later, Emma was in the dining room. To her surprise, she found herself the center of attention, surrounded by twenty girls, ranging in age from about six to sixteen, all eagerly asking her questions at the same time. She was rescued by Cora, who led her to the head of the student table, a massive, carved wooden behemoth that looked as if it could comfortably seat at least 50 girls.

As she and Cora sat down, Thora, Nedra, and several other women, Emma assumed they were teachers, trooped in and seated themselves at a small table at the front of the dining room.

"I probably should have told you this earlier, but you're the guest of honor at lunch today," whispered Cora.

"What?" said Emma, shocked. "What do you mean?"

"It's a special welcome lunch," said Cora, with a smile. "Don't worry...you don't have to make a speech or anything, but I just thought you should know."

Emma felt confused. Why were they making such a big deal about her? She was just another charity student at another girls' school. No one had ever cared so much about her at Williamson.

After a moment, Emma realized that Thora...or was it Nedra...was making a short speech about her, which was followed by student applause. Emma turned red. She wished she was anywhere else. She wasn't used to being the center of attention. She tried to smile at everyone, but failed.

"It's okay," said Cora, patting her arm. "That was the hard part. The rest of the lunch is about enjoyment! I'm sure Cook has outdone herself today. She loves celebrations!"

Cora pointed to a small printed card that was on Emma's plate. Emma looked down the long table, everyone had an identical card. She looked more closely at her card and realized that it was a menu. Was lunch like this every day? Emma felt as if she was at a fancy restaurant.

"Cook likes to make things special," smiled Cora, amused at Emma's astonishment. "You'll get used to it."

Emma nodded, looking at her menu in some confusion. Cook certainly had a whimsical way of naming food...

Emma's Welcome Lunch
Enchanted Broccoli Forest
Blushing Pear Sorbet

Blooming Pasta Primavera

Angel Cake with Berry Cascade and Whipped Cream Clouds

Based on the descriptions, Emma wasn't sure she was going to enjoy the food. It all sounded so odd! But she assumed she would have to try everything. Lunch was in her honor. She didn't want to offend anyone.

Emma looked around at the other girls in the room. Lunch was certainly a much more enjoyable affair than it had been at Williamson. All of the students were talking and laughing together. Even the instructors were chatting amiably. Everyone seemed to be having a good time. At Williamson, one of the instructors usually read an "edifying text" during meal times. Students usually ate in silence. As a charity girl, Emma was expected to help with serving meals several times per week, times that she dreaded. She was at the mercy of the other students then, and most of them didn't treat her very well. This was so different! Emma felt herself starting to relax a little.

Suddenly, the room went silent. Emma saw a small, plump kindly looking woman rolling a cart into the room.

"That's Cook," whispered Cora.

The cart was loaded with plates, and everyone in the room was oohing and aahhing over their dishes as Cook made her way around the room.

Emma received her dish and gazed at it for a moment. It didn't seem like anything special. Steamed broccoli and a few other brightly colored vegetables on a bed of salad greens...it was pretty, but nothing to get so excited about. Maybe everyone really liked broccoli?

"Isn't it lovely?" said Cora in delight.

Emma looked at her wonderingly, and then looked back at her dish. Sure it was nice...but....

Suddenly Emma started in her chair and stared at her plate in confusion.

She watched as the broccoli florets on her plate formed themselves into a tight cluster...a small forest of broccoli trees.

The "trees" spun around a few times gracefully, and then settled themselves back down on her plate.

Emma rubbed her eyes. Did that really just happen? Was she imagining things again? There had to be some explanation for what she had just seen.

Emma looked over at Cora who was happily eating her salad. "You should eat," she said to Emma. "It's really good."

Emma wasn't sure what to say. She had just seen her food move and dance on her plate. That wasn't normal! Could she really eat it?

"Sure," said Emma. Trying to push aside her fear, she took a tentative forkful of broccoli. It was the most delicious thing she had ever eaten. And she didn't even like broccoli!

"Good, isn't it?" said Cora.

"Amazing!" said Emma, almost in disbelief. "I've never eaten anything this good."

"Cook is incredibly talented," replied Cora.

The rest of the meal passed in much the same way. Each dish seemed to be possessed! The blushing pear sorbet switched back and forth from light green to a lovely sparkling pink color. The blooming pasta primavera looked normal enough when it came out of the kitchen. But after a moment, the long, thin strands of spaghetti somehow braided themselves together, encircling the vegetables on the plate. Then, to Emma's utter astonishment, the vegetables, rounds of carrots, slices of zucchini, small tomatoes, and sliced green beans, arranged themselves into a flower shape, which really did seem to be blooming on her plate.

"Cook's really outdone herself on this meal!" said Cora, as she twirled a braided strand of spaghetti on her fork.

Emma could only nod dumbly. She didn't know what to say.

"Oh dessert!" said Cora excitedly, as Cook entered the room again. "Cook is famous for her desserts!"

Emma watched as Cook began passing plates of white cake to each person in the room. When everyone had received their plates, Cook snapped her fingers and the lights in the room dimmed slightly.

Emma was riveted to what was happening on each dessert plate around her. Each piece of cake was standing upright, and, as Emma watched, a small stream of sauce, it looked like strawberry sauce, cascaded down the front of the cake, almost like a waterfall. Then, from a bowl that Cook had placed in the center of the table, a fluffy cloud of whipped cream floated over each plate, before descending gracefully down onto the cake.

Emma was mesmerized. Maybe she was going crazy, but this was fascinating!

"Watch your plate!" said Cora, pointing excitedly to Emma's dessert. "Yours is special!"

Emma looked down at her plate. She had been so fascinated by the spectacle of dessert that she had forgotten about her own. She looked down curiously, wondering what was about to happen.

The cake on her plate was the same as everyone else's, but a bit larger. As she watched, the cake seemed to sparkle and glow. Suddenly, a stream of berry sauce began cascading down the front of her cake, just as it had done for the others. However, hers was different. Three or four colors of sauce were flowing slowly down the front of her cake, creating a beautiful rainbow effect. Two fluffy clouds of whipped cream then descended onto her cake.

At this point, Emma assumed that the show must be over. But everyone was still watching her cake expectantly. Emma looked again, and to her surprise, there was a small poof and a flash, a tiny fireworks show had just erupted over her cake. In the fireworks raining down on her cake were tiny sprinkles.

Everyone in the room began to applaud, and Cook, who was standing in the doorway, blushed and nodded, clearly appreciating the attention.

"Wow!" said Emma, still amazed at what had just happened, staring incredulously at her cake.

"Eat up," said Cora, who had just started in on her piece of cake. "You don't want your whipped cream to get melty."

"Right," said Emma, still a bit dazed. It seemed like such a shame to eat what was undoubtedly a work of art....but she couldn't resist....it looked so good!

*****

The rest of the day passed in a blur. Emma accompanied Cora to a few afternoon classes that all seemed normal enough, geometry, English literature, and biology. There was no mention of witches or witchcraft. She was introduced to several of the instructors and most of the other students. Dinner was a casual affair, just soup and sandwiches...nothing like lunch! Cook, after her efforts earlier in the day, had taken the evening off and had kept things simple.

That evening, as she was getting into bed, Emma heard a soft knock on her wall.

"It's me," Cora whispered. "I told you we could chat in the evening if we both put our beds against the wall. The walls in the dorms are very thin!"

Emma was surprised. She knew Cora had mentioned talking in the evening, but she hadn't really expected it. All of the girls at Williamson used to chat and gossip in the evening, but Emma had never been of part of their group. It was strange to hear Cora's kind voice in the darkness. If anyone did try to talk to her, Emma usually just snapped at them, telling them to leave her alone or mind their own business. But somehow, she found it impossible to treat Cora unkindly.

"So," said Cora, "what did you think of your first day here?"

"Um," said Emma, not sure how to respond. "It was a bit overwhelming."

"I'm sure it was," said Cora, understandingly. "But you'll get used to it."

After a moment of silence, Cora said, "Emma, can I ask you a question?"

"Sure," she replied, wondering what Cora could possibly want to know about her.

"What was your old school like?"

Emma groaned inwardly. Williamson...the last place she wanted to think about or talk about. "Well..." she said slowly, willing herself to be honest. She had promised she was going to turn over a new leaf, and she didn't want to ruin that resolution by lying.

"It wasn't the nicest place, at least for me. I was a charity girl," she said, her face reddening with shame. She was glad Cora couldn't see her.

"You're an orphan?" said Cora, softly.

"Right," said Emma, shortly. "I never knew my parents. No one really knows what happened to them. I've just gone from one place to another since I was born. I was at Williamson for the longest time, since I was about six."

"It must have been so hard for you," said Cora.

"I guess..." said Emma. "They don't really like charity girls at Williamson...they called us chirls...and didn't treat us very nicely....

Emma trailed off. She didn't want to go into too much detail. She was only telling part of the story. She wasn't treated well, but she didn't treat the other girls or instructors well either. She was ashamed to tell Cora the entire truth. The words of Ms. Harfield rang in her ears....bully...quick tempered...mean streak.

"And why did you leave?" asked Cora.

"You mean why did I get kicked out?" said Emma bluntly.

"I didn't know you got kicked out," said Cora softly. "I'm sorry...it's okay if you think it's none of my business..."

"No, it's alright," said Emma. For some reason, Cora's kind voice made Emma feel like she could tell her story, or at least part of it. Maybe Cora would understand.

"I don't mind telling you. I got angry at one of the teachers, her name was Miss Snipes. She was always bullying the little charity girls, the ones who were too small to defend themselves. One day, she was extremely awful to a girl named Lindsay in gym class. She made her run and run until she almost collapsed. It made me so mad! That evening, at dinner, I was serving. We were having some kind of stew. I don't even remember what it was now. But instead of serving Miss Snipes, I dumped the stew over her head. I couldn't help it. I felt like she deserved it."

"Oh my goodness!" said Cora. "That's awful. But you did it for a good reason. You were just trying to help another student."

Emma wanted to tell her that there was more to it, but she couldn't. She hadn't done it just because Miss Snipes was a bully. But she felt the words of explanation die in her throat. Cora was so kind and nice. How could she tell her that she was really motivated by hatred of Miss Snipes? Emma knew that she would have done the same thing without any specific provocation. Sometimes she was mean just because she enjoyed it. It made her feel powerful and in control.

Emma sighed and said softly, "I guess so."

Chapter 4
Level 1 - Wands and Sashes

"I'm sorry you have to be with the younger girls today," said Cora, apologetically. "It's a first level class. But, before you know it, we'll be back together again."

"Sure," said Emma, uncertainly.

The past few days had been wonderful. She had taken normal classes with Cora, eaten normal meals (no dancing vegetables or floating desserts), and had started to settle into a new routine. It was so nice at the academy. And all of the girls and instructors were so nice too. It was perfect, except for the fact that everyone at the school was crazy.

Emma scowled as she noticed Samantha, the cat, who was rubbing against her leg and purring contentedly. She had been resolutely following Emma for the last few days. She seemed to have an uncanny ability to sense where Emma was going to be at any time of the day.

Cora looked at the cat and wrinkled her noise. "Samantha," she said, firmly, "leave Emma alone."

Samantha looked up at Cora forlornly. Cora gave her another firm look and then, to Emma's surprise, the cat walked docilely away.

"I've never seen Samantha take to anyone so strongly, except maybe me," said Cora, musingly, as she watched the cat retreat down the hallway. "She loves me. But she seems to be obsessed with you."

"Lucky me!" said Emma. "But I can't believe she listened to you! She doesn't listen to anyone."

"I have a way with animals, I guess," replied Cora.

"You certainly do," said Emma.

"Anyway, good luck in class today," said Cora, with a quick smile. "I know you'll do fine. And you'll learn about the sashes today," she added. "Just remember....try to keep an open mind."

Emma did her best to smile as Cora walked down the hallway. "An open mind," she mumbled to herself, as she walked into the classroom. "Does that make me crazy too?" ***

As soon as Emma entered the room, she was surrounded by eager seven year olds. For some reason, the younger girls, and even some of the older girls, treated her like a celebrity. They must not be used to new people. What else could explain her appeal?

Emma did her best to smile and chat with the girls, but she was still finding it difficult to be friendly. It just wasn't something she was used to.

Even more distracting, was the thought of witchcraft! Emma wondered about the parents of all of these girls. What were they thinking? Did they really think their children were going to learn to be witches? And why would that be something they would want?

Emma had to admit that some of the girls looked like witches. Maybe their parents didn't think there was anything else they would be able to do in life. The Rockwell twins, Annie and Amy, were the perfect examples. The girls were adorable, there was no question about it, but they did have very witchlike features. They both had identical sallow, yellowish-green complexions and tiny little matching warts on their cute button noses.

As Emma pondered these questions, Miss Weeks, the teacher of the Level I class, entered the room.

Emma reluctantly took her seat. She couldn't imagine what she was going to learn in this class. Miss Week seemed nice enough, but, like everyone else at the academy, she was nuts. She had to be, if she really thought she was a witch!

"Now girls," said Miss Weeks, "quiet down so we can get started. I'd like you all to recite the Witches Code with me."

She pointed to the board behind her, where a short paragraph was written in elaborate calligraphy.

"I don't need that," shouted one of the girls. "I already know it by heart!"

"I'm sure you'll all know it by heart soon," said Miss Weeks. "It's one of the most important parts of being a witch."

Emma rolled her eyes as the class began reciting. She mumbled along with them, but only halfheartedly. What was the point of a Witches Code? Witches weren't real!

The Witches Code:

> *Witches use their powers*
> *For good, never for evil*
> *To help, never to harm,*
> *For others, never for self,*
> *(And only when absolutely necessary.)*

Emma's mind wandered during the first part of the class. How could she pay attention to any of this nonsense? It all seemed so silly! But suddenly, her attention was attracted. Finally, Miss Weeks was talking about something that she wanted to know more about.

"Now girls, does anyone know why we wear these sashes?" asked Miss Weeks, indicating the gray sash that was tied around her waist.

"Because they're pretty?" asked Annie, one of the Rockwell twins.

"Well," smiled Miss Weeks, "that's one reason, but there's another reason that's more important."

"They're to show what kind of witch you are," said a pointy-noised girl, pompously. She seemed to be a bit of a know-it-all.

"Exactly," smiled Miss Weeks. The pointy-nosed girl was definitely the teacher's pet.

"Everyone at the academy wears a different colored sash to show their specialization," explained Miss Weeks.

"What does white mean?" Emma blurted out. She didn't want to take part in this silly conversation, but she couldn't help her curiosity.

"That's a good question," said Miss Weeks. "White basically means undecided. It's a beginner level sash. All of you are wearing white sashes since you're all beginners. Normally by the time you reach Level 2, you pick a specialty, or I should say a specialty picks you."

"What do you mean?" asked Emma, her curiosity again getting the better of her.

"Your sash will turn color, based on what type of witch you're best suited to be. It happens to all of us. And it will happen to all of you," replied Miss Weeks. "It's a very exciting event in a witches' life!"

Emma tried hard not to roll her eyes. This was all so ridiculous! Sashes that changed color...what was Miss Weeks thinking?!

One of the Rockwell twins, Amy, yelled out, "I know I'm going to have a pink sash!"

"Me too!" said her sister.

"That will all be decided in time," said Miss Weeks. "But for now, let me go over the other colors and what they mean."

Miss Weeks began writing on the board and Emma watched her closely. What a bunch of nonsense! The other girls in the room were talking excitedly about what type of witch they would be as Miss Weeks wrote.

"What kind of witch do you think you'll be?" asked one of the girls, looking at Emma curiously.

"Uh, I don't know," replied Emma, glancing at the board. She skimmed quickly over what Miss Weeks had written.

White: beginner, undecided
Brown: All-Purpose Witch (local healer, wise woman)
Pink: Magical Witch (fairy godmother, tooth fairy, etc.)
Golden Witch: Sun Witch (intermediate skills)
Gray: Moon Witch (advanced skills)

None of these options sounded interesting, especially since she didn't believe in witches. As Emma watched, Miss Weeks wrote her last ranking.

Silver: Star Witch (master, very rare)

That sounded as good as anything to Emma. She'd always liked the color silver.

"Silver maybe," said Emma. "But I haven't really thought about it that much."

The girl's eyes widened. "That's really advanced! I don't think there are any silver witches anymore! Not even Ms. Stanwick is a silver witch!"

Emma did her best not to laugh at the girl's reaction. "Well, maybe I'll be the first silver witch in a long time."

"Does anyone have any questions?" said Miss Weeks.

"What about red witches?" asked the pointy-nosed girl. "You didn't tell us about those!"

Emma's initial instincts had been right. The girl was a know-it-all.

"You've been spending too much time in the library, Jennifer," said Miss Weeks, trying to smile although her face looked troubled.

"But there are red witches, aren't there?" continued Jennifer.

"Yes, there are," said Miss Weeks. "Or, at least, there were. But that's a lesson for another time. Today, we're going to have our first lesson in witchcraft."

The girls around Emma buzzed excitedly. Emma rolled her eyes again. How was she going to get through this?

"Now, if you remember from last class, we had just gotten acquainted with wands," began Miss Weeks. She was walking around the room handing out long, thin, wooden sticks. Apparently these were wands.

"Just do the best you can," said Miss Weeks as she handed a wand to Emma. "I know this is the first time for you, so don't worry if you can't do it."

Emma nodded at Miss Weeks. This was crazy!

"Remember what I said about wands last week," continued Miss Weeks. She was now standing in front of the room, putting small objects on her desk. "Wands aren't necessary, but they do help to focus your energy when you're first learning, sort of like training wheels on a bike. Once we master each task, we won't need the wands anymore."

"So, we'll have everyone take a turn trying to move one of these objects on my desk," said Miss Weeks.

"Oh! Oh! Can I go first?" shouted every girl in the room eagerly, except Emma.

"We'll go around the room," replied Miss Weeks. "Don't worry, everyone will get a turn."

Emma couldn't believe she was sitting through a lesson in witchcraft. This was so ridiculous! Yet, despite herself, she was curious to see if anything happened.

But, Emma was to be disappointed. The girls in the class were doing their best to concentrate and move the objects on the desk, but no one could do it. For a moment, Emma thought that the pointy-nosed girl was going to be successful. It almost looked as if her object was wiggling a bit. However, despite some promise, nothing happened.

Emma was surprised when it was her turn. She hadn't been expecting to actually have to do anything. But, just as she had for all of the other girls, Ms. Weeks stood behind her and rested her hand gently on Emma's shoulder.

"And last but not least, it's Emma's turn," said Miss Weeks.

Then, she leaned over and whispered, "There's no pressure. Remember, you're just a beginner too, like everyone else. It normally takes several tries before any of the girls can accomplish much."

She paused for a moment and gazed deeply into Emma's eyes. "Take a deep breath, close your eyes, and point your wand at one of the objects on my desk."

Emma tried not to laugh. It all seemed so silly. But, she was stuck in this situation and there was nothing she could do about it. All of the other girls were watching her expectantly. She supposed it wouldn't hurt to give it a try. Her failure would just add to the evidence that witchcraft wasn't real!

Emma selected a small stone that Miss Weeks had placed on her desk. She pointed her wand towards the stone and then closed her eyes.

"Now," said Miss Weeks softly, "go to the back of your mind and concentrate all of your energy there. Push against any barriers you feel. Don't stop. Just keep going as far as you can, past the back of your mind. You'll feel it when you get there. And then focus all of your energy on the stone."

Emma almost giggled, but she tried to do as she was told. "Go to the back of my mind," she thought to herself. "Sure, whatever that means."

For a few moments, Emma felt nothing. She was trying to do what Miss Weeks had instructed, but it seemed like the back of her mind was a dead end.

But then, suddenly, something happened! It felt almost like a click, like a small door opening into another realm. She was going past the back of her mind, to another place altogether. Quickly, Emma focused all of her energy on the rock. She didn't know how long she could stay in this strange place. Then she opened her eyes.

Everyone in the room, including Miss Weeks, was transfixed by the small gray stone that was floating above the desk in the front of the room.

Emma moved her wand, and the stone made a circle around the room and then hovered for a moment over the desk.

Suddenly, Emma gasped, shocked at what she was doing. The rock fell to the table with a small thud.

"I don't know what just happened," said Emma, terrified, but elated at the same time. "I'm sorry...."

The other girls in the room were staring in Emma, in awe. Suddenly, they burst into applause, crowding around Emma and congratulating her.

Emma was speechless.

Miss Weeks looked at Emma. She seemed just as shocked as Emma was.

"I don't understand," said Miss Weeks. "Nothing like this has ever happened before. You're a natural. It's amazing!" she beamed.

Emma tried to smile back. For the hundredth time at this place, her head was in a whirl. It was hard to comprehend what was happening.

But Emma now knew....it was all real. And she was going to be a witch!

Chapter 5
Level 2 - Spells and Specialties

"Am I in trouble?" asked Emma, apprehensively, as she pushed Samantha off her lap. The pesky cat would not leave her alone. Samantha meowed pathetically and then stalked haughtily off.

Emma was nervous. She had been summoned to see Thora and Nedra in the study that morning. She wasn't sure what she had done wrong, but it must be something serious. Why else would they want to see her?

Emma was perched on the edge of the couch, looking anxiously from Thora to Nedra, who were seated across from her.

"No, of course not," said Thora, reassuringly. "We're just a bit surprised, that's all."

"What you did in your first witchcraft class has never happened before," added Nedra. "No one ever moves an object on their first try. And you were able to do it perfectly. It's astounding!"

"I'm shocked too," said Emma. "I didn't think ANY of this was possible! In fact, I thought you were all crazy, until yesterday."

"We know," said Nedra, kindly. "And we don't blame you for it. Anyone who has never seen the workings of witches before would think the same thing."

"But how did you do it?" asked Thora, curiously.

"I don't know," answered Emma honestly. "I just did what Miss Weeks said. I pushed as far as I could to the back of my mind, something sort of clicked, and then I was able to move the stone."

"Amazing," said Nedra. "That's exactly how it happens, but normally it takes a long time to learn."

"It's not a bad thing, is it?" asked Emma, suddenly worried. "I didn't break any rules, did I?"

"No, no," said Thora, "of course not. You actually did something incredible! You should be proud of yourself."

"I don't know if I can be proud yet," answered Emma. "I'm still having a little trouble understanding everything."

"It'll take time," said Nedra, "but you'll get used to it, don't worry."

"The reason we asked you here this morning," said Thora, "is to see if you'd like to speed up your learning process. We both think that you could probably skip most of the Level 1 classes and go right to Level 2. Miss Weeks said she'd give you a condensed version of Level 1 skills. And then you'd be ready to start Level 2. "

"We don't want to rush you," added Nedra, "but we think you're more than ready. And you'll be with girls closer to your own age. If you keep going at such a quick rate, you'll probably be caught up with Cora very soon. She's just started Level 3."

"Sure," said Emma, her head in a whirl. She had no idea what Level 1, 2, or 3 meant, but if Thora and Nedra thought it was a good idea she wasn't going to argue. "Whatever you want me to do."

"Wonderful!" said Thora, with a large smile. "You're going to love your Level 2 classes!"

*****

The next week passed quickly. Emma was given a crash course in Level 1 skills by Miss Weeks.

"Go easy on yourself!" Ms. Weeks kept telling her. "You're learning in a few days what it takes most students years to master."

But Emma couldn't slow down. She was having too much

fun.

By the end of the week, Emma was a competent Level I witch.

She could make an object levitate, move an object from place to place, at various speeds and altitudes, and make objects appear and disappear. But Emma's favorite was the most difficult task, "transforming" one object into another.

"It's actually a bit of an illusion," explained Miss Weeks. "You're really switching two objects, not changing them. But it looks very much like a transformation to someone who's not in on the secret."

Emma nodded as she concentrated on "changing" a spoon into a fork.

"But why do we have to put the items back at the end?" asked Emma, after she had successfully switched her spoon and fork. "It ruins the illusion."

Miss Weeks smiled, as she chanted, "Always put things back in their proper places." She had drilled this rule into Emma's head during their lessons.

"Witches always clean up after themselves," continued Miss Weeks. "It's one of our cardinal rules. You'll learn that soon enough!"

*****

"As all good witches know, we have been cruelly misrepresented throughout history," said a small, neat woman, who was standing in front of the classroom.

She pointed to a screen behind her which depicted a stereotypical witch...an ugly hag, green-faced, warty, wearing a shapeless black dress, pointy black hat, and clutching a broom.

Emma was sitting in her first Level 2 class, The History and Ethics of Witches, taught by Miss Addams, the official historian of Witches Academy.

Emma was fascinated. Everything she thought she knew about witches was wrong!

Miss Addams waved her hand and the image on the screen behind her changed. Now it was showing a historical scene clearly out of some nightmarish past. There was a large crowd gathered and a woman was about to be burned at the stake.

"Besides being misrepresented, witches have also been persecuted throughout history, blamed for events and tragedies in which they had no involvement. Witches, and by default, women, have been used throughout history as scapegoats for every possible misfortune. When events were not understood, something or someone had to be found to take the blame."

Ms. Addams waved her hand again, and the screen behind her changed to show a group of women, all dressed in gray and wearing gray sashes, clearly graduates of Witches Academy.

"But, unlike this inaccurate historical portrayal, witches are actually remarkable, talented, and brave women. Instead of being responsible for the terrible events of the past, we have been charged with protecting humankind. Our job is to help people, not harm them. We are protectors, not persecutors. Our spells and powers are only used for good. We never cast evil spells or put curses on people."

Ms. Addams paused for a moment and then smiled proudly. "Witches are noble and powerful women, and that is exactly what you are all going to become at Witches Academy."

*****

Emma's next Level 2 Class was called Basic Spell Casting. She wasn't sure what to expect and she was a bit nervous. Moving objects had been easy enough. But casting spells? That seemed much more complicated.

"There are ten basic spells," explained Ms. Waverly, the Level 2 spell instructor, at the beginning of the first class. "Once you master these spells, you will be able to make your own spell combinations. Spell casting is the part of witchcraft where you can be creative and make use of your own unique talents. The better the witch, the stronger her spells."

Ms. Waverly, a tall, young woman with a commanding voice, took a large box from under her desk.

"Each of you will receive a spell book. From now on, you will use this book to keep track of all of the spells you learn in this class, as well as to store the spells that you create on your own. These books are very valuable, so please, guard them well."

As Emma watched, Ms. Waverly removed the first spell book from the box. To Emma, it looked like a very high tech smartphone.

"Cell phones?" Emma said, incredulously.

A younger student named Maggie looked over at Emma and smiled.

"Sort of," she said. "They're like regular cell phones, but they've been upgraded for witchcraft."

"I didn't know witches were so high tech," said Emma, wonderingly.

"Miss Stanwick likes to keep us up to date on everything. We always have the latest and greatest inventions here, explained Maggie. "Witches love technology," she added, as if reciting a mantra.

"I can see that," said Emma, as she was handed her "spell book" by Ms. Waverly.

"Now," began Miss Waverly, "let's start with Spell #1, binding ....."

*****

A few weeks later, Emma was talking to Cora before they both went to bed for the evening.

Cora was perched on Emma's bed, smiling at her new friend.

"It's incredible how quickly you've picked everything up," she said. "I think you'll be able to join me in Level 3 soon, which will be wonderful."

"It seems like a dream," said Emma. "Just about a month ago, I didn't know witches even existed. And when I got here, I thought you were all crazy. But now, I'm learning to be a witch."

Cora laughed. "It's funny isn't it? You didn't believe in witches, and now you're going to be the most talented witch ever!"

Emma blushed and then looked a little uncomfortable. She still wasn't sure about so many things. And having so much power...she wasn't sure she trusted herself with it. In some ways it worried her.

Cora looked at closely. "Are you alright?" she asked.

"Of course," said Emma quickly. "It's just that this is all a little overwhelming."

"It's a lot to learn in a short time," said Cora, understandingly.

Emma nodded and tried to smile.

"Have you learned all of the spells yet?" asked Cora curiously.

She paused for a moment, and then said, in a perfect imitation of Ms. Waverly, "The ten basic spells are binding releasing, soothing, joining, sundering, increasing, decreasing, muddling, mending, and healing."

"Almost," laughed Emma. "We've heard Miss Waverly repeat them over and over, just like that. We're on number eight right now. But I think we'll get through the rest pretty quickly."

"I know you will," said Cora. "You're amazing!"

Emma was surprised by Cora's reaction to her newfound talents. She didn't seem to be the least bit jealous. In fact, none of the girls were. Emma didn't understand it. No one at Williamson would have reacted like that. They were all so competitive. Emma had always worked hard to be the best at Williamson. But no one had ever been happy about her success. Instead, she had always felt as if the other girls at the school were her rivals.

"You look worried again," said Cora, patting her friend on the arm. "There's a lot going on in your head, isn't there?"

"Sorry," said Emma. "I'm not used to having anyone to talk to. I've always dealt with things on my own."

"You know you have someone to talk to now, right?" said Cora.

"I know," answered Emma, with a smile.

"You don't mind if I ask you something Cora, do you?" said Emma, suddenly. "It's something I've been wondering about."

"Ask me anything," said Cora. "I don't have any secrets from you."

"By the end of Level 2, everyone's sash has turned color to show their specialty. But your sash is still white. You're so far along. Why hasn't your sash changed yet?"

Cora blushed and looked very uncomfortable.

"I figured you would be wondering about that," she said with a sigh. "I know I promised to tell you on your first day here, but it's not something I like to talk about. It's so awful and embarrassing. All of the women in my family are gray witches. And I'm not. I don't know what I am! I feel like I'm letting everyone down."

"I'm sure your sash will turn soon," said Emma, reassuringly.

Cora sighed again and looked away. She struggled for a moment, as if trying to make a decision. Suddenly, she got up and walked quickly into her dorm room. In a minute she was back in Emma's room, holding a few wadded up sashes.

"I haven't shown these to anyone," said Cora, anxiously. "But I feel like I need to tell someone. And I trust you."

Cora spread out the wrinkled sashes on Emma's bed. They were a beautiful opalescent blue-green color that shined strangely in the dim light of the room.

"They're beautiful!" said Emma.

Cora looked at her ruefully. "They might be beautiful, but what do they mean? There's no such thing as a blue-green witch! I'm supposed to be a gray witch, but my sashes keep turning this color!"

Emma looked at the sashes in wonder. "There has to be some explanation," she said. "Have you thought about asking Thora or Nedra?"

Cora shook her head vehemently. "I'm too ashamed to tell anyone! What if it means I'm not even supposed to be a witch?"

Emma shook her head slowly. "I don't think that's true for one minute."

"Really?" said Cora, with a hint of hope.

"Really," replied Emma. "We're going to figure this out together."

"That would be nice," said Cora, softly. "Maybe between the two of us, we can make me into a gray witch"

"A gray witch," said Emma, "or something even better!"

Chapter 6
The Practice Room
and the Dance

"And this is the practice room," said Miss Camber, the instructor of Advanced Spells for Level 3 students.

As she spoke, she indicated a heavy door in the central hallway of the school. Emma had walked by this door before, on her second day at the school when Cora had given her the "grand tour."

"Why is it so....secure?" asked Emma, searching for the right word. The massive door looked as if it was the entrance to a well-guarded fortress.

"The spells that the students learn in Advanced Spells can be a bit....unpredictable," answered Miss Camber.

"We've found it's better to have a layer of protection," she added.

As if to underline her words, there was a large crash, followed by a brief flash of light. Emma jumped, but Miss Camber seemed undisturbed.

"Don't worry...that's just Esmerelda," said Miss Camber.

"Oh!" answered Emma. She remembered that Cora had mentioned Esmerelda on their tour. Emma had met Esmerelda a few times. She was the oldest student at the school, and had been struggling for some time to pass her third level exams. But, judging by the sounds coming from the practice room, it didn't seem as if she was making much headway.

After a moment, the door opened and a tall, clumsy looking girl appeared. She was a bit singed, but otherwise, unharmed.

"How did it go this time?" asked Miss Camber

"Not too good," answered Esmerelda, with a smile. Despite her lack of success, she seemed to be in good spirits.

"Hi Emma," she smiled, noticing Emma standing behind Miss Camber.

"But I do think I'm getting closer," continued Esmerelda. "If I could just get that last spell to cast correctly I think I could pass the test."

"Well, keep trying," said Miss Camber, encouragingly. "I'll know you'll get it eventually."

Esmerelda walked off down the hall, singing to herself, and Miss Camber smiled at Emma.

"Let me show you the practice room," she said, taking Emma by the arm. "You're going to be spending a lot of time down here in the next few weeks, so we'll get you familiar with your new home. You've mastered the ten basic spells, but now you have to learn how to combine them. And that can be a little dangerous!" ****

"But why do I have to go to the dance at all?" asked Emma yet again, as Cora held up one dress after another, trying to find the perfect one for her friend.

"Everyone is going!" said Cora. "It's the Halloween dance! It's a big deal!"

Emma groaned. She'd never enjoyed dances. Her old school used to host several dances each year with a neighboring boys school, and for Emma, they were always a nightmare. She never had anything to wear, was laughed at by the other girls, and was usually a wallflower for the whole evening. She didn't have much experience talking to boys her age, and she always felt stupid and awkward.

"I don't like dances," Emma tried again. "I never have. I'd much rather stay here and practice my spells."

"Don't be such a nerd," said Cora, holding up another dress to Emma. "I know you'll have a good time. You just have to give it a chance."

"What do you think of this one?" said Cora, holding up a

sparkling burgundy dress. "I think it would look amazing on you."

"Whatever you say," said Emma. "It's not as if I really care."

"Oh but you should!" said Cora. "You want to look nice, don't you?"

"I guess," said Emma doubtfully.

Cora sighed. "Well, you're going to look nice whether you want to or not!"

"Who are we trying to impress anyway?" asked Emma.

Cora blushed and smiled. "No one in particular," she said, quickly.

"The boys at the wizard's school aren't really the cream of the crop," she continued, as she began fussing with Emma's hair. "Wizardry is nothing like witchery! Wizards are mostly just a bunch of geeks who can do a few magic tricks. But, there are a few wizards who aren't that bad. Plus you can meet my cousin Winthrop. He's a total dork, but nice all the same."

"I can't wait," said Emma sarcastically.

*****

To her surprise, Emma was having a good time at the dance. She'd never been to a dance which she had enjoyed, but somehow this was different.

She and Cora were standing by the refreshments table, surveying the crowd of people in the room. The dance had been going on for about an hour or so, and it seemed as if everyone was enjoying themselves, including the teachers.

Cora was absentmindedly fiddling with some of the party decorations, large pots of mums that were arranged down the length of the table. As Emma watched, the mums seemed to grow slightly larger and took on a healthy glow, as if they were enchanted by Cora's presence.

"What did you just do?" asked Emma, curiously, as she watched the mums sparkle.

"Huh?" said Cora. "I don't know what you're talking

about."

Before Emma could reply, she was distracted by a boy who was unsuccessfully attempting to execute a complicated dance step in the middle of the dance floor.

"Ugh," groaned Cora, following Emma's gaze. "My cousin Winthrop is such a nerd!"

"You could have told me that he was cute," said Emma.

"Winthrop!" said Cora, in shock. "Cute!"

"Yeah," said Emma. "He's good looking."

"You can't be serious," said Cora in disbelief.

"I guess you only have eyes for Gandalf over there," said Emma, with a laugh.

Cora blushed again, just as she had earlier that evening. Across the room, a tall boy with dark, messy hair and dark eyes, dressed in a black robe, was performing an elaborate spell, to the delight of a small crowd of female onlookers.

"His name is Gavin Knightley," said Cora, still blushing. "And I don't know why he's dressed like that. But he does like being the center of attention."

"Clearly," said Emma, looking at the group of admirers around Gavin.

"I suppose it's because it's Halloween," said Cora. "Maybe it's his costume."

Emma rolled her eyes and took Cora by the arm. "Come on," she said. "You're going to lose your chance if you don't act fast."

"What do you mean?" said Cora, looking nervous.

"I mean," said Emma, "that if you don't go ask Gavin to dance right now, you're never going to be able to dance with him tonight. Look at all of those other girls! They're your competition."

Cora paled. "I can't ask him to dance. I've never said more than two words to him."

"Well, it's about time you started being a little more talkative. You forced me to come to this dance...one of us better dance with someone!"

With that, Emma tightened her grip on Cora's arm and dragged her across the room to where Gavin was standing.

Gavin had just finished another trick and was basking in the glow of admiration.

Emma cleared her throat loudly to attract his attention.

"Hey," he said, looking towards Emma with a frown. He was clearly upset that she was interrupting his show. "You must be the new girl. I don't think we've met."

"I'm Emma," she said. "And I think you've met my friend Cora before."

Gavin's annoyance noticeably softened at the sight of Cora. "Of course," he said, with a mock bow. "No one could forget the beautiful Cora."

Cora's already pink face deepened about three shades.

"Right," said Emma, with a small smile. She pushed her friend towards Gavin and then said, "I'm going to go get something to drink. I'll see you two later."

Emma walked off, smiling to herself. Cora would thank her later. And it served her right! If she didn't want to be bossed around then she shouldn't have made Emma come to the dance with her.

After a moment, Emma paused and looked back. The two were walking towards the dance floor, Cora with a lovely smile on her face.

"A job well done," said Emma to herself.

Emma turned to walk back towards the refreshments table, but, before she could get very far, she collided with someone who was standing directly in front of her.

"I'm so sorry," she said, trying to disentangle herself. "Oh! It's you, Winthrop."

Emma had been hoping she would get a chance to talk with Winthrop that evening. He seemed interesting, although maybe not the best dancer.

"That's okay," said Winthrop. "I was trying to get your attention. Everyone's been talking about you around here. You're the amazing new witch!"

Emma smiled despite herself. She couldn't figure out why Cora didn't like about Winthrop. She looked at him more closely as he began talking. He was tall and a bit awkward looking with red hair and a freckled face. Perhaps he was a bit nerdy, but she couldn't help thinking that he was cute.

"I've been wanting to show someone my latest innovation," said Winthrop, as he pulled a cell phone out of his pocket. "If you're as good as they say you are, you'll definitely appreciate it."

Winthrop's phone looked like the ones used at Witches Academy. She looked at Winthrop curiously. This wasn't exactly what she'd expected, but she couldn't help being interested.

"Look at this," said Winthrop, as he swiped a few screens on his phone. "I've developed a new way to organize spells. If you use my program, you can cast spells almost three times as fast."

Emma was instantly entranced. She could see what Winthrop had done and it was brilliant, yet so simple.

"That's incredible!" said Emma. "How did you think of doing that?"

"I'm a bit of a computer nerd," said Winthrop, with a slight smile, "at least that's what Cora would say."

"Well," replied Emma, "being a computer nerd is a good thing if you can make spell casting easier. What else have you done on that phone? I'd love to see some of your other improvements."

"You would?" said Winthrop, sounding slightly surprised. "I have lots of things I could show you, if you're really interested..."

Winthrop swiped a few more screens and then frowned. "Sorry, this is going to take a few minutes. You haven't noticed any problems with your phone lately, have you? I keep running into little glitches that just don't seem normal."

"Some of the witches have been having minor problems lately," replied Emma. "But I think it's just because we need to run some updates, at least that's what our spell instructor told us."

"I don't know," said Winthrop, doubtfully, as he continued to fiddle with his phone. "This seems like more than just an update..."

Just then, Emma noticed Cora glaring at them from the dance floor. She waved her hand, as if she wanted them to join her.

Emma looked at Winthrop and smiled. "I think Cora wants us to dance," she said.

Winthrop looked up at his cousin. "She's annoyed at me!" he said, in delight. "She thinks I'm keeping you here talking about nerdy stuff when we should be dancing."

"I like talking about nerdy stuff more than I do dancing," said Emma.

"Me too," laughed Winthrop in agreement.

Before they could join Cora and Gavin on the dance floor, there was a pause in the music and one of the wizard instructors walked to the center of the room.

"I'm sorry to interrupt the dancing," he said, "but we're ready to start the annual wizard Halloween competition." By this time, Cora and Gavin had made their way over to where Emma and Winthrop were standing.

"What's he talking about?" asked Emma.

Cora smiled and said, "Wait until you see! It's the best part of the evening!"

"We'll see you later," said Winthrop. "Gavin and I have to get ready for the competition."

Gavin looked at Cora and smiled. "I always win," he said. "But this year I'll win for you."

As the two walked away, Emma glanced over at Cora and rolled her eyes. "You really like him?" she asked, incredulously.

Cora blushed yet again. "I know he seems full of himself," she said. "But he does have a lot of good qualities. You just have to give him a chance."

Emma nodded, unconvinced.

"So what's this competition all about?" asked Emma, curiously.

"They do it every year," said Cora. "It's a chance for the wizards to show off their skills. They have to build castles, or at least illusions of castles. But, while they're building their own castles, they can also attack the other castles being built. Whoever has the last castle standing wins the competition."

"Oh," said Emma. "This should be interesting!"

"It certainly will," said Cora. "Let's get a good spot. I want us to be able to see everything."

Emma and Cora walked to the center of the room where the crowd had gathered. They made their way as close to the front as they could, and then waited expectantly.

In a few moments, a group of about ten wizard students, including Gavin and Winthrop, had gathered in a line. There was a hush among the crowd as the contest began.

Emma watched in amazement as the boys began working their magic. Before each student, a glimmering castle began to take shape. It was obvious how talented each boy was by the speed with which his castle was constructed and by its overall beauty.

It was an incredible spectacle! Emma was mesmerized by how quickly castles were being constructed, and, even more so, by how quickly they were being destroyed. Several students, whose castles were very impressive, were almost immediately out of the contest because their castles fell prey to the attacks of their fellow students.

After a few moments, it was obvious that the contest was going to be between Winthrop and Gavin. Soon they were the only two left. Each was working furiously to gain the upper hand. Winthrop's castle was smaller than Gavin's, but it was much more detailed and exquisitely beautiful. Gavin, whose castle kept getting larger, with battlements and towers being added every few minutes, didn't seem as interested in the finer details. His castle was impressive, but to Emma, it didn't show the same skill in construction and taste as Winthrop's. Part of

66

the reason for this lay in the fact that Gavin was directing most of his attention to attacking rather than to constructing. Winthrop, who was engrossed in beautifying his castle, was barely defending himself against Gavin's attacks and not mounting any of his own.

Emma didn't understand why Winthrop didn't attack. She wanted him to win. She was ready to attack Gavin herself!

"Watch out Winthrop," whispered Emma. "He's going to get you if you're not careful!"

She could see Gavin gathering his energies to mount his largest attack on Winthrop. And, in a moment, it was all over. Gavin waved his arm dramatically, there was a flash, and Winthrop's beautiful castle was gone.

Everyone gathered around Gavin to congratulate him. Cora, who seemed torn between comforting her cousin and congratulating Gavin, was quickly pulled away by Gavin himself, who wanted her to pose with him for pictures in front of his winning castle.

Only Emma remained to comfort Winthrop.

"Your castle was beautiful," she said, as she walked over to him. "It was so much better than Gavin's. But why didn't you attack his castle? I'm sure you could have beaten him if you'd tried."

Winthrop smiled. "I wasn't playing to win. I just wanted to build an amazing castle. I think it matters more to Gavin," he said, gesturing towards the crowd. "He loves this kind of stuff!"

Emma looked over and tried not to smile. Gavin was striking dramatic poses in front of his castle, clearly reveling in all of the glory and the attention.

"I suppose you're right," she laughed in agreement.

Chapter 7
The Test

Emma was sitting in the study of Witches Academy where she had first arrived two months ago. It seemed like an eternity now. So much had changed!

She caught herself absentmindedly petting Samantha, who had sneakily settled next to her on the couch. She was so caught up in her own thoughts that she hadn't really noticed the cat.

"Ugh," she said, as she pushed Samantha off the couch and onto the floor. "I wish you would leave me alone!"

As she disentangled herself from the devoted cat, Thora and Nedra entered into the room.

"Sorry we made you wait," said Thora. "There was a small problem in the kitchen. Cook went a little overboard in her preparations for dinner this evening. Unfortunately souffles aren't her specialty. We had to help with the cleanup."

Emma smiled. She had gotten used to the fascinating array of magical dishes that came from the kitchen, some not quite as successful as others.

"We haven't had a chance to congratulate you on all of your successes," said Nedra, with a soft smile. "You've made us very proud!"

"It's not often that one of our students is able to do what you've done," said Thora. "You've passed through years of schooling in a few months! It's really remarkable!"

Emma blushed, despite herself. She wasn't used to praise and it still made her feel a bit uncomfortable.

"Thank you," she said, humbly. "It's still hard for me to

believe too."

"That's understandable," said Nedra. "So much has happened."

"But I think you're here to talk about the future," said Thora. "Or at least, that's what we assumed."

"Yes," said Emma, a bit nervously. "I've come to a decision. Or I guess I should say a decision has been made for me."

"And what would that be?" asked Nedra.

Emma pulled her sash out from under her school blazer. She held it towards Thora and Nedra so that they could see the strip of gray that was beginning to recolor the white sash.

"I noticed it last night," said Emma.

Thora and Nedra beamed at her.

"I can't say we're surprised," smiled Thora. "We've been expecting and hoping for this for some time."

"It's the only thing for someone as talented as you," nodded Nedra. "And it will be so wonderful for the academy and witches in general! You're a wonderful example for all of us!"

Emma smiled. She was surprised at how happy Nedra and Thora seemed to be.

"What am I supposed to do now?" she asked.

"Oh of course," said Thora. "Being new here, you probably don't know all of the steps."

"First, you have to see the head of the academy, Ms. Stanwick. She gives you an evaluation, just to make sure you're ready to continue."

Emma felt a shadow of annoyance pass over her face, but she tried to conceal it. Everything she'd heard about Ms. Stanwick made her nervous. Why wasn't she ever at the academy? Some of the girls said she was high and mighty in her ways. Emma didn't want to be examined by someone like that!

"Once that's completed," said Thora, "you'll be given one more task, a Quest, which you must complete before you can become a full-fledged gray witch."

"A Quest?" asked Emma. "What does that mean?"

"It's different for everyone," said Nedra. "And yours will be just as unique. But that's something that will be decided when you see Ms. Stanwick. She's the only one who can assign you a Quest. She'll know what you need to do."

Emma wondered. A Quest? It sounded so strange! She had more questions, but something else was uppermost in her mind at that moment. Emma was worried about her meeting with Ms. Stanwick. She wanted to prove that she was ready to be a gray witch. She didn't want to embarrass herself.

"How do I study for my evaluation with Ms. Stanwick?" asked Emma.

"It's not really something you can study for," replied Nedra.

"Don't worry," said Thora, with a resassuring smile. "We wouldn't let you go through with the evaluation unless we knew you were ready."

Emma returned Thora's smile half-heartedly. Somehow, she didn't feel reassured. ***

"Where is she?" said an impatient voice loudly. "This better not be a waste of my time! Do you know how busy I am? And when was the last time we had a real gray witch? I can't remember it was so long ago!"

"She's waiting in your office," said Nedra, gazing apprehensively at Ms. Stanwick.

Nedra always forget what a whirlwind Ms. Stanwick could be. Today seemed to be a particularly stressful day for her.

"It's alright," said Nedra, placing her hand on Ms. Stanwick's arm. "You're not going to be disappointed. "Emma isn't like anyone I've ever seen before."

Ms. Stanwick seemed to soften slightly. She sighed deeply before speaking again. "It's always so nice to be back here with you at the academy. I forget how peaceful it is here. The world outside....it's not like this."

"I know," said Nedra, patting Ms. Stanwick's arm again. "It's good for you to be here. You'll have a chance to relax a little."

"Perhaps I need it," smiled Ms. Stanwick as she walked into

her office to meet Emma. ***

Emma had been waiting for about five minutes in Ms. Stanwick's office, trying unsuccessfully not to be nervous. She didn't know what to expect. A test she couldn't study for and a head witch who was said to be harsh and impatient! How could she not be nervous?

Emma gazed around at Ms. Stanwick's office, trying to distract herself from her worries. Just like all of the other rooms at the academy, this one was richly furnished and beautifully appointed. A massive mahogany desk dominated the entire room. Somehow, the desk made Emma feel even smaller and more anxious.

Emma's examination of her surroundings was cut short by Ms. Stanwick's abrupt entrance. She gazed at Emma as she entered the room, and then walked over to her desk, her heels clacking loudly on the hard floor.

"You must be Emma," she said shortly.

"Well, there's not much to you," she added, as she looked Emma up and down.

Emma was already nervous and Ms Stanwick's brusque manner put her on the defensive. Despite her best intentions, she felt angry. She wanted to snap at Ms. Stanwick, but she tried to control her temper. Instead, Emma took a deep breath and sat silently, looking at Ms. Stanwick warily.

In appearance, Ms. Stanwick was stunning, perhaps even a bit awe inspiring. She was very tall and thin and dressed elegantly in a gray suit. She had the palest skin Emma had ever seen, but she didn't look unhealthy. Her hair, which was jet black, was pulled back loosely, and made her seem even paler. She had incredible eyes, deep gray and piercing.

Ms. Stanwick picked up a file on her desk and started flipping through it.

"Your performance here has been very impressive," she said.

"Thank you," said Emma.

"That's not a compliment," Ms. Stanwick replied. "Lots of

girls are able to master the spells, although perhaps not as many as quickly as you. That's only the surface of being a witch. The real test is what's within."

Emma didn't say anything, but she felt her anger rising again. Was Ms. Stanwick trying to insult her?

"I'd like to ask you a few questions, if you don't mind," she said.

"Of course," said Emma, feeling a sense of relief. They were finally getting to the test. Now at least Emma could show Ms. Stanwick what she knew.

"How long were you at Williamson?" Ms. Stanwick asked.

Emma was taken aback. She had expected questions about the skills that she had mastered over the last few months, not about her past!

"Most of my life," said Emma, reluctantly. "I was at one other place before Williamson...a foster home when I was very young, but I don't remember it that clearly."

"No memory of your parents then?" asked Ms. Stanwick.

Emma cringed. The thought of her parents was painful. She only wished she had some memory of them. "No," said Emma. "Nothing."

"And have you always been a bit of a bully?" Ms. Stanwick continued.

Emma stiffened. "I'm not sure what you mean," she replied stiffly.

"Your record at Williamson makes it clear that you didn't always get along with the other girls," said Ms. Stanwick. "You did a lot of things that strike me as cruel."

Emma reddened and snapped, "They only got what they deserved!"

She paused for a moment, and took a deep breath, trying to rein in her anger.

"I'm sorry," she said. "My time at Williamson isn't something I like to talk about. I haven't always been the person I'd like to be. The girls at Williamson weren't very nice to me, and I wasn't very nice to them. I'm trying to be better here."

"And how's that going?" asked Ms. Stanwick.

"It was going fine until I started talking to you!" Emma blurted out.

Emma hadn't intended to say what she was thinking out loud, but Ms. Stanwick had made her so angry. Emma glanced at Ms. Stanwick nervously, uncertain what her reaction would be.

To Emma's surprise, Ms. Stanwick smiled and began laughing, a delicate, silvery laugh that made Emma smile in return.

"You certainly don't mince words," said Ms. Stanwick. "But really, besides dealing with me, how are you getting along here?"

Suddenly, Emma felt the urge to lie creep over her. She wanted to tell Ms. Stanwick that everything was easy and she'd already changed her ways. But she couldn't. Somehow, she knew that even if she tried to lie, Ms. Stanwick would see right through her.

"It's okay," said Emma, slowly. "But it's easy here. Everyone's so nice. Plus, I've been so busy learning how to be a witch, that I haven't had much time for anything else."

Emma paused for a moment, and then said, quietly, "But I know that my first impulse still isn't to be kind."

"Thank you for being honest with me," replied Ms. Stanwick. "That's a good quality."

Ms. Stanwick was silent for a few moments, as she wrote some notes on the papers on her desk. Then, she stood up and walked towards Emma.

"Now, let me get a better look at you," she said.

Ms. Stanwick took Emma by the arm and raised her up from the chair where she was sitting. Then, she looked down into Emma's face. Her gray eyes, which suddenly struck Emma as understanding rather than judging, looked into her own eyes for a very long time.

"There's more to you than I thought," Ms. Stanwick said

finally, "much more, so much potential, so much untapped power. I haven't seen anyone like you in a very long time."

Ms. Stanwick paused and then her gaze clouded slightly, "But there's darkness in you too," she said, gazing at Emma with compassion. "That makes the power you command very dangerous."

Emma turned her head away. "I know," she said, almost in a whisper.

"Your Quest will show whether you can overcome your darkness," said Ms. Stanwick.

Emma looked at Ms. Stanwick in surprise. "Then I passed the test?" she asked, in disbelief. "You didn't even ask me any questions"!

"Oh," said Ms. Stanwick, with a dismissive wave of her hand. "Of course you passed. I can't turn someone like you away. And I did ask you a lot of questions. You may not have been aware of all of them, but you told me much more than you think.

Emma smiled in spite of herself. Her interview with Ms. Stanwick had been unnerving. But, despite the ordeal she had just gone through, she was happy. She was one step closer to being a gray witch!

Chapter 8
The Quest

"Your Quest starts here!" said Ms. Stanwick, majestically, as she led Emma towards the entrance to the library.

Emma felt a slight sense of disappointment as she stood in front of the library door. The library! She had pictured something much more exciting. Weren't Quests supposed to be full of adventure?

"Have you been in the library before?" asked Ms. Stanwick.

"No," replied Emma slowly. "I almost came in once, but Cora thought it was better we didn't go in alone."

"Well, she was right," said Ms. Stanwick matter of factly. "It is haunted, after all."

"Haunted!" repeated Emma, in surprise.

"Is it safe to go in?" she asked, as Ms. Stanwick began to open the door.

"Of course it's safe," scoffed Ms. Stanwick. "Witches are more powerful than ghosts."

Ms. Stanwick paused for a moment as she turned the door knob, "You just have to be careful as you come in and out," she said.

Ms. Stanwick opened the door a crack, just enough for them to squeeze through. She then pulled Emma through the door with her, closing it quickly behind them. Just as they entered the room, there was a loud whooshing noise, followed by a crash.

"Duck!" said Ms. Stanwick. As she spoke, there was a thud against the wall right above their heads.

"Foiled again!" said an angry voice.

"Oh Knight," said Ms. Stanwick in exasperation, "stop being so dramatic!"

Instead of an answer, a large pile of books came flying through the air towards them. Just as they were about to be hit, the books stopped in midair, rearranged themselves into a neat triangular shape, then fell to the floor with a clatter.

"I do hope you're going to put those away," said Ms. Stanwick, in annoyance. "You know these books are old. You shouldn't be throwing them around."

Suddenly, a shape began to materialize in front of them. To Emma's fascination, a figure of a tall man appeared, a knight dressed in a full suit of sparkling green armor. He was tall and regal, but had a gloomy air about him, as if he were filled with sadness.

"You shouldn't boss me around then," retorted the ghostly man. "The treatment I receive here is terrible!"

Ms. Stanwick sighed in frustration. "You know you're welcome to leave at any time," she replied.

The knight glared at her angrily. "You know what would happen if I tried to leave. You shouldn't say things like that to torment me."

The knight turned away from Ms. Stanwick to look curiously at Emma. "I haven't seen you before. Are you going to introduce me old Stanwick? Or have you forgotten all of your manners?"

Ms. Stanwick sighed and looked from the knight to Emma. "I suppose the two of you should get acquainted, since Emma is going to be spending some time here.

"Emma, this is the Lost Knight. He lives in our library. He's been here forever, and, unfortunately for us, I doubt he'll ever leave. He should leave you alone while you're working, but if you have any problems let me know."

"I do have a name," said the knight, imperiously. "It's Sir Horatio Higginbotham.

Then he looked at Emma more closely. "You don't seem that bad," he said. He paused for a moment and then sighed despondently. "But I'm sure you'll turn against me, just like they all do."

Emma smiled slightly and put out her hand to take that of the knight's. "I'm very glad to meet you, Sir Horatio," she said, sincerely. Despite her earlier apprehensions, the sight of the knight had greatly lessened her fears. Emma had been picturing an ugly, angry, bitter old witch haunting the library, not this slightly sad man.

The knight looked at her in surprise, as if not used to such politeness. His face turned a bit red, and then he disappeared, without another word.

"Oh he is a nuisance!" said Ms. Stanwick. "But we can't get rid of him! At least he's gone for now! You can see he's no one to be afraid of...but anyway, on to more important matters..."

As Ms. Stanwick spoke, she took Emma by the hand and walked her to the center of the room. The library, which Emma had scarcely noticed before due to the distractions caused by the Lost Knight, was magnificent. The room was several stories high and the walls were lined with dark wooden bookcases, all filled to overflowing with new, old, and ancient texts. Emma had never seen anything so incredible.

"This will be your home for the next few weeks," said Ms. Stanwick, as she waved her arm around to take in the whole room. "Here you will discover your Quest!"

Emma glanced around the room, uncertainly. There were thousands upon thousands of books. How was she supposed to find her Quest here?

"But how?" said Emma, slightly dismayed.

"Amongst the books of course," said Ms. Stanwick, "this is a library after all."

"But there are so many," replied Emma. "Am I supposed to read them all?"

Ms. Stanwick smiled at Emma and led her towards a large table in the center of the room. "Not exactly," said Ms. Stanwick. "We are in the 21st century, after all. And remember, witches love technology."

As Ms. Stanwick spoke, she ran her hand lightly along the edge of the wooden table. As she did so, the surface of the table took on a rippling, water-like quality. From the center of the table several large screens materialized.

"All of the books are here," said Ms. Stanwick, motioning towards the screens. "You don't have to do anything more than sit here and scan."

"Oh," said Emma, slightly less daunted, but still overwhelmed. Although she wouldn't have to take each book down off the shelf, she would still have to search through them all.

"But even with all of the books at my fingertips," said Emma, gesturing towards the screens, "how am I supposed to discover my Quest? What am I even looking for?"

"Don't worry," said Ms. Stanwick, as she led Emma over to the table, pulling her down into one of the chairs. "You don't have to find your Quest....your Quest will find you."

She took Emma's hand and placed it on one of the screens. "All you need to do, is let it!"

As Emma's hand brushed across the screen, it exploded into a pattern of swirling light and color. After a moment of searching, a group of results appeared on the screen.

"These results are specifically matched to you," said the Ms Stanwick. "Your Quest is here, waiting for you. All you have to do is figure out what it is!"

*****

"I give up," said Emma in frustration. "I'm never going to find what I'm looking for! I've been here two weeks and I'm no closer to finding my Quest than I was when I started!"

Horatio, who was hovering above Emma, looked at her sympathetically and said, "Of course you'll find it. It's just going to take a little more searching."

"Well, I'm tired of searching!" replied Emma. "Maybe I should just be a brown witch. It would be much easier!"

"You can't do that!" said Horatio, floating down towards her and perching on the desk next to her. "You're destined to be the greatest gray witch ever! I know it!"

"I don't know what I would do without you," Emma said, looking up at Horatio's transparent face with affection.

Horatio smiled at her, a ghostly grin lighting up his face.

"I never thought I'd be friends with a ghost!" laughed Emma.

"I never thought I'd be friends with a witch," replied Horatio. "You're the first witch who's ever been nice to me!"

Emma smiled as she thought about her unexpected friendship with Horatio. He was certainly not what she had expected, or what she had been led to believe by the other witches. From what they had told her, Horatio was a menace, tormenting anyone who entered the library. But, Horatio was nothing like that! He was kind, thoughtful, and caring. He had helped her immeasurably over the past weeks.

Emma had also learned much of Horatio's sad history. He had a wife and seven children that he hadn't seen in a very long time. His courageous exploits were recorded in several of the books in the library, as well as tales of his generosity and kindness. Many, many years ago, he'd been pulled from the pages of history by a novice witch's spell gone wrong. Ever since, he'd been trapped in the library, with no hope of ever returning to his old life and family.

Emma was determined to help him get back to his own time...as soon as she figured out her Quest.

"Anyway, if I read this page one more time, I'm going to go crazy!" said Emma. "I don't understand why the computer keeps showing me this one particular page. It doesn't have anything to do with anything related to me, at least not that I can see."

Horatio looked at Emma kindly. He wanted her to succeed, but he was just as much in the dark as she was.

"I've gone through all of my original results so many times...to get nothing!" continued Emma. "And then, when I try to narrow down my results, all I get is this one page, and it's ancient history! What does it have to do with me?!"

"Maybe if you read it out loud?" suggested Horatio. "You haven't tried that yet."

"I doubt that will help much," said Emma, half-heartedly. "But I suppose it's worth a try. At this point I don't know what else to do.

Emma sighed and focused her attention on the scanned page that the computer kept showing her. She must have read it at least one hundred times already.

"In the year 1347," Emma began, "the Black Plague spread death and destruction over Europe. The people were in despair and moods were dark..."

Emma's voice flagged as she continued reading. She didn't think she'd be able to reach the bottom of the page.

"As everyone knows, the Red....

Emma paused for a moment and then stopped.

Horatio looked at her, "Well...go on," he said. "You're right in the middle of the sentence."

"But that's where this page ends," said Emma. "Do we have to keep going? I think I'm going to fall asleep."

"At least finish the sentence," suggested Horatio.

Emma touched the screen and the page turned. "As everyone knows, the Red....Plague had dire consequences."

Emma stopped for a moment, not sure she had read correctly. "Hmmm," she said. "I didn't notice that before."

"What?" said Horatio, who, despite his best efforts, had only been half listening to Emma's reading.

"When I turn the page and read the whole sentence, it says the Red Plague," she answered. "But this is a history of the Black Plague. There's no such thing as a Red Plague! I think there's something missing."

Emma leaned in closer to the computer screen. She went back to the previous page and looked at it more closely. "This page is numbered 1010," she said. "But the next page is numbered 1012. We're missing a page!" she said, the excitement rising in her voice.

"Do you think this is what I've been looking for?" said Emma. "Do you think I've finally found the key to my Quest?"

Horatio smiled. "I'm not sure, but I know how to find out. Having lived here for almost one hundred years, I know this library like the back of my hand!"

He floated above Emma and held out his hand. "Follow me....we'll figure this out together."

Chapter 9
Discovery

"This better be good!" said Ms. Stanwick, impatiently. "This is the second time you've dragged me away from work this month. Don't you realize I'm a busy woman with things to do?!"

Emma was clutching a book tightly to her chest. This time, she wasn't annoyed at Ms. Stanwick's abrupt manner. Instead, she felt small and insignificant. The weight of what she had discovered made everything else seem unimportant in comparison.

Thora and Nedra, who were also in the room with Emma and Ms. Stanwick, both began speaking at once.

"Oh no!," said the two together.

"This isn't a waste of your time!" said Nedra.

"You'll see why we called you away. Just give Emma a chance to explain," added Thora.

Ms. Stanwick, softened slightly by Thora and Nedra's reassurance, did her best not to glare at Emma, as she said, "Alright then, tell me."

Emma took a deep breath and set the book down in front of her. Her voice felt a bit shaky, but she tried to quiet her fears as she began her story.

"Yesterday, in the library," began Emma, "I came across a mistake in one of the books I've been looking through. I realized that one of the pages hadn't scanned properly into the computer. So, I went and found the book."

Ms. Stanwick looked at Emma curiously and then at Thora and Nedra. "How is that even possible?" she said slowly. "The witches used their spells to scan those books," she said. "There's no way they could have missed a page."

Nedra looked at Ms. Stanwick apprehensively and said, "I think there might have been some interference, but let Emma continue her story."

Emma opened the book she had been clutching. "This is the page that was missing," she said. "I'll read you what it says..."

Emma began reading, in a nervous voice that sounded nothing like her own.

"The Red Plague will be a repeat of the Black Plague, but on a much larger scale. In the time of troubles, the Red Witch will return. She will gather her forces to spread death and destruction. 672 years after the onset of the Black Plague, the Red Plague will begin. But there is hope. The Red Witch can be stopped by an untested witch, but only by one who has felt the lure of the dark paths."

Emma stopped reading and let her words sink in. "If you do the math, the year that's mentioned...it's now," she said.

Ms. Stanwick was looking at Emma intensely. It was clear that she was disturbed.

"I don't understand any of this," said Emma. "I didn't even know there was such a thing as a Red Witch until yesterday!"

"I suppose we might as well tell you, since you know so much already," said Ms. Stanwick. "It's not really a secret, but it's something we don't always explain until there is a need. And, over the past few centuries, there hasn't been a need. We all thought the curse of the Red Witches was over. But it seems that they were just biding their time..."

Ms. Stanwick sighed and looked at Emma sadly.

"Red Witches are Gray Witches that have fallen," she continued. "They've gone against the tenets of the Witches' Creed. Instead of only using their power when needed, for good and helping, and for others, Red Witches use their power for their own ends. They usually start out believing that they're doing good by bending the rules. But they always turn to evil in the end. Once one rule is broken, the others fall away quickly. Red Witches are responsible for many of the tragedies that have beset the human race...wars, disasters, and illnesses."

So a Red Witch caused the Black Plague?" asked Emma.

Ms. Stanwick nodded slowly. "Yes," she replied. "And from what this book says, it's clear that another plague is being planned. A spell must have been cast on this book a long time ago, so that the warning was hidden from all of us, until now."

Emma sat in her chair silently for a few moments, trying to understand everything Ms. Stanwick had said. She felt a deep sadness within herself. Witches had been the only people she'd known thus far that were untouched by anything bad or evil. And now, she was learning that this wasn't true.

"But why did the book find me?" said Emma, wonderingly. "I'm not the first witch who's had to undergo a Quest in all of the years since the Black Plague. I don't see what I have to do with any of this. I just got here. I'm still a beginner...."

"Don't you see?" said Ms. Stanwick.

"No," said Emma, beginning to feel even more nervous and confused than she already did.

Ms. Stanwick took the book from the table in front of her. She found the spot she wanted and began reading, "The Red Witch can be stopped by an untested witch, but only by one who has felt the lure of the dark paths."

Emma looked at Ms. Stanwick, still not sure that she understood.

Finally, realization dawned on Emma. "You can't mean me!" she said, in shock.

Ms. Stanwick nodded her head slightly. Emma looked around at Thora and Nedra, hoping they would contradict what Ms. Stanwick had said. But they only gazed at her mournfully.

"But I can't!" said Emma, confusion turning to anger. "It's not possible! And I don't know anything about dark paths! Just because I'm not always perfectly kind and nice doesn't make me the person you're looking for!"

Emma paused for a moment, and then shouted, "I don't even know if I want to be a Gray Witch anymore! And I certainly don't have to fix your problems! I'm not responsible for any of this!"

Emma stormed out of the room, angry tears blurring her eyes. She was done with this place. She thought she had finally found a home. But she had been mistaken.

Chapter 10
Decisions

Emma was busy throwing her few belongings together. She had to leave. She knew she had nowhere to go, but she didn't care. She couldn't stay at the academy any longer.

"Hey," said a soft voice behind her.

Emma started. She hadn't heard Cora enter her room.

"Hi," said Emma shortly, continuing her haphazard packing.

"What are you doing?" asked Cora, gently.

"What does it look like I'm doing?" snapped Emma. "I'm leaving...getting out of this awful place. I'm not a witch and I should have never tried to be one."

"Is this about your Quest?" asked Cora.

"My Quest!" laughed Emma derisively. "What a ridiculous thing that is! My Quest is to save the entire world from the Red Witch! I only just learned about witches a few months ago, and now I have to save them. Well, they can find someone else. I'm not doing it. It doesn't make any sense!"

"It's your Quest," said Cora simply. "It's not supposed to make sense."

"You're just as bad as the rest of them!" snapped Emma, whipping around to glare at her friend. "They all seem to think I should do this! They're all crazy!"

Cora looked at her kindly, "I know this must all seem like a lot to take in, but I know you Emma, I know you can..."

Emma interrupted her angrily. "A lot to take in, that's an understatement! And no Cora! You don't know me! I'm not like you...all good and kind and perfect!"

Cora started. Emma's words had touched a nerve. She got up and turned as if to go, and then paused.

"Just because you're not like me doesn't make you bad," said Cora, softly.

Emma looked at Cora for a moment her eyes flashing angrily. Then, her face changed. Tears started to her eyes and she turned away.

Cora touched Emma on the arm, but Emma still wouldn't look at her.

"I'm sorry Cora," said Emma, struggling through her tears. "But you don't know me. I'm not good...I wish I was more like you. I haven't told you everything about me..."

"There's nothing you could tell me that would change what I think about you," said Cora.

"Yes there is," said Emma. As she spoke she turned to face Cora directly. Her face was flushed and her eyes were still filled with tears, but she spoke more steadily.

"What I told you about my time at the other school....not all of that was true. I did do a lot of things to protect the other girls. But it wasn't just to help other people. I...." Emma hesitated, and then took a deep breath before continuing, "I liked being mean. I enjoyed getting revenge on the girls and the teachers...and not just the ones that did something bad to me. There's something in me...something that's not good...and I can't always control it..."

"We all have good and bad in us," said Cora. "It's part of life."

"But not like this," said Emma. "This is more."

"I understand," said Cora. "I can see it in you. But that's the point of the Quest...to choose the path of good or evil."

"That sounds like witches' wisdom," said Emma with a slight smile.

"It is," said Cora, with a returning smile. "It's on page 11 of the Witches Guide to Proper Behavior."

Emma sighed, her smile fading as quickly as it came. She paused for a moment, and then said, almost in a whisper, "I'm scared Cora. I don't know if I can choose the good. It's not always easy for me. That's why I don't want to do this Quest."

"If you don't face it now, you're going to have to face it at some time...it's not going to go away," replied Cora.

Emma sighed again and looked at Cora. "I guess I already knew that. But it seems much easier to run away."

"You won't run away," said Cora, confidently. "You're not like that. And you're not alone. Witches stick together. You'll have lots of help on your Quest, especially from me."

"Thank you," replied Emma softly. "I know I can't do this alone."

Chapter 11
Black Witches

Emma sighed in frustration. Despite her fears, she had committed to undertake her Quest. But, after a week, she felt as if she was still no closer to figuring out what she was supposed to do than she had been when she started.

She was sitting in the library, listlessly scanning through the same books, just as she had at the beginning of her Quest. She knew what the Red Witch planned to do, she just didn't know how. How was she supposed to find out? Ms. Stanwick, as usual, seemed to think that the library was going to show her the way, but there was nothing that Emma could find in any of the books that was helpful.

"What am I supposed to do?" said Emma, in annoyance. "Should I just keep sitting here looking through dusty old books while the Red Witch sets her plan in motion? My Quest is going to be over before I've even started it!"

As Emma spoke, Horatio materialized next to her. Emma hadn't seen much of him in the past few days.

"I was starting to think you were mad at me," said Emma, with a smile, happy to see her friend.

"No," said Horatio, a small smile lighting up his melancholy face. "I wasn't avoiding you. "I've been busy trying to figure out how to help you."

"Did you find anything?" asked Emma, eagerly. If no one else, perhaps Horatio could help solve her quandary.

"Yes" said Horatio slowly. "It's not the answer to your question, but at least I can point you in the right direction. I think I know who can help you."

Emma looked at Horatio curiously as he slid his pale translucent fingers over the computer screen.

"This is what you need," said Horatio, pointing to the image of a book that had just appeared on the screen.

"A History of Black Witches," read Emma. She groaned, "There are Black Witches too! Why don't they teach us any of this in school! Just last week I learned about Red Witches, and now suddenly there are Black Witches! What else am I going to find out?"

"If you read this book," said Horatio, "you'll see why Black Witches aren't mentioned. They're certainly not as bad as the Red Witches, but they're not something that proper witches want to advertise. They're sort of like the black sheep of the witch world."

Emma sighed, "I'll read this too, but I don't really see how it's going to help me."

"It will," said Horatio, confidently. "First, you need to learn what a Black Witch is," said Horatio. "That's where the reading comes in. Then you need to find one....that part might be a little harder..."

"Everything seems to be hard right now," sighed Emma, as she began to read.

*****

Later that evening, Emma was sitting with Cora in her room, telling her what she had learned in the library.

"Where am I supposed to find a Black Witch?" asked Emma, earnestly. "I didn't even know there were Black Witches until today. And now I'm supposed to find one to help me on my Quest!"

Cora blushed and looked at Emma closely. "You're sure it's a Black Witch that you need?"

"Yes," said Emma, looking at her friend curiously. "Why? Do you know one?"

Cora's blush deepened and she looked away from her

friend. "I actually do," she replied, hesitantly.

"Why didn't you say something before?" said Emma, excitedly. "All of our problems are solved!"

"It's not quite that easy," said Cora slowly.

"Well, knowing a Black Witch is better than being completely in the dark! Who is it?"

"Do you remember when you met my parents when they came to visit?" asked Cora.

"Of course," said Emma. "How could I forget? They were so nice. They treated me like I was their daughter."

Cora smiled. "Well, they would do that. But that's not important right now. Do you remember when the conversation turned to my Aunt Ethel?"

"Yes," said Emma, thinking. "Someone mentioned her and everyone got very quiet."

"That's because she's a Black Witch," said Cora. "The family is ashamed of her."

"From what I read, Black Witches don't seem that bad..." began Emma.

"Of course they're not that bad," replied Cora. "At least not in the way that Red Witches are, but they're still witches that have chosen the wrong path. They're not necessarily evil, but they're not all good either. They go against much of what witches stand for. If you'd been brought up in a family of witches you'd understand a little more. Black Witches bring an entire family down. That's why no one ever speaks of them."

"I think I understand," said Emma. "But I don't think we have a choice. We need to go see your Aunt Ethel. She's the only one who can help us."

"I suppose you're right," said Cora, reluctantly. "But we need to be very careful. Black Witches, especially my Aunt Ethel, can be dangerous. They won't give anything away without asking for something in return. And we can't tell anyone we're going. They wouldn't let us if they knew."

"Don't worry," replied Emma, "it'll be our secret."

Chapter 12
The Trip

The next day, Emma and Cora were seated in the back seat of Gavin's large, luxury SUV, on their way to Aunt Ethel's house. Emma wasn't thrilled about spending most of the day in Gavin's company. But they didn't have a choice. He was the only person they knew who had a car. Luckily Cora had invited Winthrop as well. Hopefully he'd make the trip more bearable.

Cora's aunt lived about an hour's drive from Witches Academy. But, as Cora had warned them, it wasn't going to be easy to find her. Black Witches didn't like to be bothered by people from the outside world. And they chose their dwelling places accordingly. Aunt Ethel lived in the middle of a forest. The road to her house twisted and turned and doubled back, playing tricks on any who were brave enough to attempt it.

"You're sure this is the right way?" asked Gavin, for about the hundredth time. "I feel like we're going in circles."

"We are going in circles," said Cora. "But that's the only way we'll be able to find Aunt Ethel's house. We have to keep driving around until she feels like letting us in."

Gavin groaned as he maneuvered his car around another large rut in the middle of the road. "I wish your aunt was a little more friendly!"

Cora smiled slightly. "Black witches aren't known for their hospitality."

"I think I see something!" said Winthrop, suddenly. He was pointing straight ahead of them, into what looked like a thick outcropping of trees.

"Where?" said Gavin, in annoyance. "I don't see anything but more trees."

Emma strained her eyes in the direction that Winthrop was pointing. At first she couldn't see anything but the same trees that seemed to be crowding in about them from every side. But then, after a few moments, the trees started to fade and she could see a small clearing with a house standing in the middle.

"There is something there!" said Emma.

Cora sighed in relief. "Thank goodness," she said. "I wasn't sure if we were going to be able to find it at all. Sometimes Aunt Ethel can be very difficult."

Gavin pulled his car to the edge of the clearing and parked. He gazed anxiously through the shifting trees and then looked at Cora.

"You're sure this is a good idea?" he asked, as the two girls began to get out of the car. "I don't want anything to happen to you, Cora."

Emma stifled a laugh. Apparently Gavin didn't care what happened to her!

"Don't worry, Gavin," said Emma. "I won't let anything happen to Cora."

"And, if we're not back in half an hour, don't come looking for us," added Cora. "Just leave and get help. Thora or Nedra will know what to do."

"We can't leave you out here!" said Gavin, in protest.

"Cora's right," said Winthrop. "We're no match for Aunt Ethel. Last time I saw her, she threatened to turn me into a toad! And she wasn't joking. I don't think she likes me."

"Don't worry," smiled Cora. "We won't let Aunt Ethel turn anyone into a toad today. But we will tell her you said hi. You are her nephew, after all. And hopefully she'll be in a good mood today."

"I hope so," said Winthrop, earnestly. "Aunt Ethel can be nice, when she feels like it."

"We'll see. You never know what you're going to get with

Aunt Ethel," said Cora.

*****

Cora and Emma walked cautiously around the trees at the edge of the clearing. As soon as they entered the clearing, the trees began shifting again. Emma looked back nervously, only to see that the trees had closed the path behind them, completely blocking her view of Gavin's car. When she turned around to look towards the house, the trees had shifted again, cutting off their way forward.

"Uh, Cora," said Emma, "do you think your Aunt Ethel might be trying to tell us something?"

Cora shook her head and smiled slightly. Then, she put her hand out and touched one of the trees, speaking softly to herself as she did so.

As soon as she touched the tree, the shifting stopped. The trees were suddenly out of their way, and there was a clear path to the small house in the clearing before them.

"What did you just do?" asked Emma, in wonder.

"Nothing," said Cora, looking at her friend in surprise. "Why?"

Before Emma could respond, Cora had begun walking quickly towards her aunt's house.

"Let's hurry," said Cora, "before something else happens!"

Emma rushed after her friend, and the two scrambled onto the front porch of the house together.

*****

A few moments later, Emma and Cora were sitting comfortably in Aunt Ethel's warm, cozy kitchen.

The situation was very far from what Emma had expected. In fact, she still felt a bit stunned.

Emma knew that Black Witches can be very unpredictable. One day, a Black Witch might be harsh, mean, gnarled, old, and ugly. And the next day, depending on her whim, she might be young, glamourous, kind and caring. Emma and Cora had gotten lucky. They had picked a day for their visit when Aunt Ethel was feeling pleasant and domestic.

Aunt Ethel had taken the guise of a lovely, older woman. She was tall, slim and energetic, with perfectly coiffed silver hair and an elegant silk dress. Her house, which had appeared a bit rustic from the outside, was nothing like that on the inside. In fact, faultlessly decorated, it matched Aunt Ethel's domestically elegant manner.

As Cora and Emma looked on in wonder, Aunt Ethel bustled about the kitchen, pulling out fancy china plates and cups.

"If only I'd known for sure that you were coming," said Aunt Ethel, "I'd have made things a little nicer."

There was already what looked like a feast assembled on the kitchen table, piles of fancy cakes and petit fours, heaps of fancifully iced cookies, and a massive fruit tart as a centerpiece.

"This is more than enough," began Cora.

"Oh Cora," interrupted Aunt Ethel with a sigh. "Let me look at you! You're even lovelier than I'd imagined. You've grown so much since I saw you last. I wish you'd come to see me more often..."

Cora looked uncomfortable. "I'm sorry," she began, "but...."

"Oh I know," said Aunt Ethel, with a dismissive wave of her hand. "All of those stuffed shirts won't let you come here, not to see Aunt Ethel! I'm the shame of the entire family, a horrid Black Witch!"

Emma looked at Aunt Ethel curiously. Despite herself, she couldn't help but ask a question. "But I don't understand. You seem so normal!"

Aunt Ethel looked at Emma and laughed. "What a funny thing to say. Of course I'm normal, but I've gone against the way of the witches. And they don't like that. They've made me an outcast so no one else follows in my footsteps!"

"So maybe Black Witches are a little eccentric," continued Ethel, "but we like to do things our own way. I don't think that makes us bad. We're independent. We don't like to take orders from a head witch, or anyone else for that matter."

Emma nodded. She could understand the feeling. She didn't like to take orders from anyone either. In fact, she liked to be the one in charge.

"I realized a long time ago that things in this world aren't always as simple as following a little code," said Aunt Ethel. "Sometimes the code doesn't work, and I've had to do things that aren't approved by the higher ups. But I'm certainly not someone to be shunned, like a Red Witch! The way Ms. Stanwick talks sometimes you'd think there isn't any difference between Red Witches and Black Witches. But there is! Red Witches break the rules and they can't stop. They're so tempted by power that they turn evil. Black Witches only bend the rules. We know when to stop and we certainly aren't evil."

Emma felt herself relax a little. She was beginning to like Aunt Ethel. Maybe this woman would be able to help her.

Aunt Ethel stopped speaking and looked at Emma. "But what am I doing, babbling on like this? You're here because you need something from me."

Emma blushed and looked a little bit confused. "Well..." she said, not sure how to begin.

"It's okay," smiled Aunt Ethel, reassuringly. "I know all about you and your Quest. I know you need my help."

"I'm not exactly sure what to ask you," said Emma, hesitantly. "We know what the Red Witch is planning. But we don't know where she is or how to stop her."

"And that's where I come in!" said Aunt Ethel, with a smile. "Black Witches are good for a few things!"

Aunt Ethel snapped her fingers, and the entire room transformed around her. Instead of a cozy kitchen and a table packed with treats, Cora and Emma were now seated at a large round table which was supporting a giant crystal ball. The room had become quite dark, and only a few candles flickered around them. Even Aunt Ethel had changed. Her hair was now jet black and flowing and she wore a long black gown.

Aunt Ethel sat between Cora and Emma and put her hands on the crystal ball.

"And now for the fun part," said Aunt Ethel. She closed her eyes and mumbled a few words.

Suddenly, the crystal ball flashed brightly. For a moment, it looked as if it was filled with a swirling mist, and then images began flashing rapidly across the surface of the orb.

Emma could hardly make out what she was seeing. It was all moving so fast!

After another moment, the ball turned black and then the room plunged into darkness.

Emma heard Aunt Ethel snap her fingers, and suddenly, the room was filled with light again. Everything, including Aunt Ethel, were how they had appeared when Cora and Emma first entered the house.

"Well, said Aunt Ethel, as she readjusted her perfect hairdo, "that was fun girls, wasn't it?"

"Did that help you figure anything out?" asked Emma, wonderingly.

"Oh yes, of course!" said Aunt Ethel. "I always forget that they don't teach you how to use crystal balls at Witches Academy. It's really quite a waste. They're so useful for so many things!"

"What did you see?" asked Cora, curiously.

"Lots of things," said Aunt Ethel, with a mysterious smile, "but only two of the things that I saw are helpful for Emma and her Quest. First, the Red Witch is in the Stone Tower in the Place Between. And second, Winthrop, that delightful nephew of mine, is going to help you stop the Red Witch. In fact, he already knows what she's doing, he just doesn't realize it."

"Winthrop!" said Cora, in shock. "What does he have to do with any of this?"

"You'll see," said Aunt Ethel.

"And what's the Place Between?" asked Emma. "I never heard of that before."

"Another thing they should teach you about," said Aunt Ethel, with a sigh. "Your education is really lacking. Ms. Stanwick will be able to explain it to you. She knows all about it, and how to get there."

"So, is that everything?" asked Emma. "Isn't there more you can tell us?"

"I know it doesn't seem like a lot," said Aunt Ethel, "but don't worry. You have everything you need now."

Emma nodded, still not sure she understood everything that had just happened. "Thank you for your help," she said.

"It was my pleasure," Aunt Ethel said, as she stood up. She smiled and walked closer to Emma. Then, she put her hands on Emma's shoulders, and looked deep into her eyes.

"You're even more wonderful than I thought you'd be," she said.

Emma felt a bit frightened. Aunt Ethel seemed to be looking into her soul.

"So much power...but something else too..." she continued, thoughtfully.

"I know," Emma replied, in a whisper. "There's darkness in me. I don't know if I have the strength to overcome it."

"No one knows, until they're tested," replied Aunt Ethel, gently. "But you're powerful. You have the strength to prevail. And now you have this too. It will help, when you most need it."

Aunt Ethel held out her hand and suddenly a small, wrapped package appeared in it.

"This is for you," she said, handing the item to Emma.

Emma looked at it curiously. "Thank you," she said, as she took it in her hand.

"You don't have to open it now," said Aunt Ethel. "But keep it safe."

"And now," said Aunt Ethel, with a sigh. "I know you must be going. Those boys out there will be getting restless."

Aunt Ethel waved her arm and a large box appeared in her hands.

"Here," she said, giving the box to Cora. "Winthrop and Gavin might appreciate some of my baking."

"I'm sure they will," smiled Cora. "Especially Winthrop...he's convinced you still want to turn him into a toad. This will make him feel better!"

"Thank you so much for your help and your hospitality," said Emma, as they walked to the door.

"We'll come back and see you," added Cora.

"If you can," said Aunt Ethel. "I know how hard it is for you to come see me."

"And Cora," she added, looking intently at her niece. "Don't let anyone make you take the wrong path."

"What do you mean?" asked Cora, in surprise.

"You're not a pink witch or a brown witch or a gray witch, or any of those other silly colors," said Aunt Ethel, firmly. "You're made from much finer material."

"But there aren't any other options," said Cora.

"Oh yes there are!" said Aunt Ethel, with a nod of her head. "There's a special path for you. You'll find it soon, don't worry."

*****

Emma and Cora walked towards the car slowly.

"That was not at all what I expected," said Emma.

"You never know what to expect with Aunt Ethel," replied Cora. "But that was a pretty amazing visit!"

Emma nodded, her head in a whirl. Aunt Ethel had given them so many clues, but she still couldn't make sense of all of the pieces.

As they walked away from the house, Emma glanced down at the ground below them. There, under Cora's feet, small white flowers were blooming.

"Look!" said Emma, in surprise. "They're beautiful!"

Cora looked down and smiled. "Aunt Ethel must be doing

it!"

Emma looked back at the house, which had taken on a darker aspect in the few minutes since they'd left.

"I don't think so," said Emma, wonderingly. "I think it has something to do with you!"

Cora laughed dismissively. "Don't be silly," she said. "I'm not doing anything."

As soon as Emma and Cora reached the car, Gavin hopped out and opened the door for them.

"Was everything okay?" he asked. "We were starting to get worried about you!"

"We're both fine," said Emma, with a smile. She was fairly certain Gavin hadn't been worried about her!

"Was she as awful as she was last time I saw her?" asked Winthrop.

"Not quite as bad," smiled Cora, as she handed the box filled with sweets over to Winthrop. "She wanted you to have these. And there was no mention of turning you into a toad this time.

Winthrop opened the box and pulled out a large pastry. "Yum!" he said, as he took a bite. "Maybe I should have gone in with you!"

Winthrop handed the box to Gavin who looked at it suspiciously without taking anything. "More importantly than pastries, did she tell you what you need to know?" he asked.

"She told us enough to get us started," replied Emma. "But the most important thing she told us is that we're supposed to ask Winthrop how to stop the Red Witch."

"Huh?" said Winthrop, looking at Emma in confusion.

"You hold the key to this whole mystery!" said Emma. "Tell us what to do!"

Chapter 13
The Grand Council

"Could everyone please quiet down so we can get this meeting started?" said Ms. Stanwick, her strong voice cutting into the anxious murmuring that filled the room.

There were several hundred witches seated expectantly in the Great Hall of Witches Academy. All of the various witches, grey, brown, pink, and gold were represented. Witches had come from all over the world to be at this council, and there was a nervous energy in the air.

"I think most of you know why I've summoned you here," began Ms. Stanwick, as soon as the room was quiet enough for her to speak.

"The Red Witch is active again. We haven't faced a catastrophe like this in a very long time. We're going to be tested like we have never have been before, and we need all of you to help."

"Our young witch here," Ms. Stanwick nodded towards Emma, who was seated on the dais behind her, "is going to give you a brief summary of what has been going on and what we need to do. This is her Quest."

Emma was a bit surprised. She knew that Ms. Stanwick wanted her to explain her discoveries, but she hadn't realized that she was going to take on such a leading role. Wasn't she still only a student? It was a little scary to be given so much responsibility. And the other witches were so accepting of Emma's position. She was so much younger and less experienced than them. But it seemed that her Quest singled her out and made her different.

Emma nervously approached the podium. She wasn't used to speaking to large groups of people, especially ones that were so distinguished. Emma cleared her throat a few times, and then began speaking, trying to project a confidence she didn't feel.

"A few weeks ago," said Emma, "as part of my Quest, I came across a strange passage in one of our histories in the library. The passage indicated that a Red Witch would return at this particular point in time with a new weapon. The book indicated that the weapon would be similar to the black death, that devastated Europe in the Middle Ages."

There was a gasp in the room as the witches digested this information. Most of them knew that the Red Witch was again threatening, but they didn't know all of the details.

"The Red Witches claim responsibility for the earlier plague. However, since it wasn't as successful as they had intended, they're trying again now. But this time, they're much more technologically advanced. They'll be using techniques that are going to be difficult for us to overcome."

"Some of you may have noticed your phones acting strangely lately. We all just assumed that this was a normal glitch that would be fixed in time. But it's not. Winthrop, one of the wizards at our neighboring school, has been helping us with the technological aspects of the problem. He discovered that the Red Witch is planning to use cell phones to infect people with a newer, much deadlier version of the plague, the Red Plague. In fact, the virus has already been spread. Anyone who has a phone is already a carrier. Luckily, it hasn't been activated yet. But we have to stop the Red Witch before she puts her plan into action. And we don't have much time."

Emma finished speaking and stepped aside. Her nervousness had quickly decreased as she started talking. There was passion, conviction, and a bit of fear in her voice. The gravity of what she was saying had spread over the entire room.

Ms. Stanwick stepped forward again. "Thank you Emma,"

she said graciously. "You now know what we are up against. We have a plan in place already, thanks to Emma and Winthrop. Tomorrow, we battle the Red Witch. The gray witches, led by me, will proceed to The Place Between to face the Red Witch and her army. Emma will accompany us."

"Unfortunately, we aren't as vibrant as we once were," continued Ms. Stanwick gravely. "Our numbers have declined over the years and, as you can see, there aren't many young faces in the room. However, I believe that our strength and skills will prevail, regardless of our numbers."

"While we are battling the Red Witch, the remaining witches will help the student wizards rid our phones of the Red Plague. If we are successful against the Red Witch, our spells will spread quickly, removing the plague from all phones. It will take a very large effort to cast all of the necessary spells, so we need all of you here working as hard as you can."

"Is that understood by everyone?" asked Ms. Stanwick, her voice suddenly sounding very tired.

There was a murmured yes throughout the room.

"I wish we were gathering under better circumstances," said Ms. Stanwick, as she gazed around the room sorrowfully. "But, if we are successful, our reunion after the battle will be a celebration."

*****

Later that evening Emma and Cora were sitting in Emma's room.

Neither of the two girls could sleep. They knew what the next day would bring, and it was hard not to be fearful.

Emma was holding a small object in her hand. "What is it?" she asked Cora, curiously.

Cora looked at the object, a bit fearfully. "Is that what my Aunt Ethel gave to you?"

Emma nodded. "It's beautiful, but I have no idea what it

is."

"It's a black knot," said Cora, slowly. "I've never seen one before. You're right, it is beautiful, but it's dark magic. It can be very dangerous."

"Why?" asked Emma. "What am I supposed to do with it?"

"Every witch will use it differently," said Cora. "But it's supposed to give you influence over the people around you. If the witch is very powerful, she can control others using a black knot. I assume my Aunt Ethel thought you'd need it when you face the Red Witch."

Emma looked at the black knot gravely, then she placed it carefully on her desk.

"Are you going to bring it with you tomorrow?" asked Cora.

"I'm not sure," said Emma, thoughtfully. "I don't know if it would help or make things more difficult."

Cora looked tearfully at Emma. "I wish I could go with you," she said. "I didn't know Ms. Stanwick was only going to let gray witches go."

"You are coming with me," Emma replied. "I need your help."

"But you heard what Ms. Stanwick said today," said Cora. "Only gray witches are allowed. And I'm not a gray witch. I still don't know what I am!"

Emma smiled slightly. "I have a surprise for you," she said.

"What is it?" asked Cora, curiously.

"Horatio and I did some research after we saw your Aunt Ethel," said Emma, mysteriously. "And I think we found something."

Cora looked at her friend in confusion. "I have no idea what you're talking about," she said.

"Have you ever heard of an Earth Witch?" asked Emma.

"No," said Cora, shaking her head.

"Well" replied Emma slowly, "you should know about them, because that's what you are!"

"I don't understand," said Cora.

"There's a lot of interesting witch history in the library," smiled Emma. "In fact, there are several volumes devoted entirely to Earth Witches."

"I don't think there's such a thing as an Earth Witch," said Cora, doubtfully. "I'm sure I would have heard of them by now."

"You might think that," said Emma. "But not many people know about Earth Witches. They're very special and very rare. They only arrive when needed, and hundreds of years can pass before an Earth Witch appears. But you're an Earth Witch! I know it! And we need you, especially now."

"But how do you know?" asked Cora. "I don't see how you can be so sure."

"You're the exact description of an Earth Witch," said Emma. "Listen to this..."

Emma pulled a book from her desk, opened it to a page she had marked, and began reading:

"Earth Witches have a special connection with nature, including animals, plants, trees, and especially flowers. They have a unique bond with the world around them. Every living thing responds to their presence with joy and renewed life. Earth Witches are beautiful, kind, and gentle. Flowers are known to bloom under their feet."

Emma paused in her reading, and said, "That's happened! I've seen it!"

"I don't know," said Cora slowly, still skeptical. "I'm not that special."

"Yes you are!" said Emma. "You're incredibly unique!"

"But what am I supposed to do?" said Cora. "What do Earth Witches do?"

"Normally, they protect and care for the earth," said Emma. "But sometimes they're called on to do more. Tomorrow, I need you to help me. You're coming with me and the gray witches. I need your help to defeat the Red Witch." ***

Emma found sleep next to impossible. She had talked with Cora for quite some time and then both girls had gone to bed.

She could hear Cora breathing peacefully in the room next to hers. If only sleep would come to her! But she knew it wasn't going to happen anytime soon. She had too much on her mind.

Emma carefully got out of bed, trying not to make any noise. She made her way slowly out of the dorm room, doing her best not to bump into anything in the almost total darkness. The school was completely silent, everyone long since retired.

Emma made her way to the library, hoping that Horatio would be there to talk to her. True to her hopes, he was hovering about the door as she entered the room, almost as if he had been waiting for her.

"I knew you'd come," he said, his mournful visage almost looking happy at the sight of her.

Emma smiled at him. Despite her worries, his presence always made her feel better.

"I couldn't sleep," said Emma. "I have too much on my mind."

"I can understand that," replied Horatio gravely. "Tomorrow is an important day."

Emma looked at Horatio and then away. "I know," she said. She wasn't sure what she wanted to say to him, but she felt as if he might be able to help her in some way.

"You're afraid," he said simply.

Emma flushed, at first feeling angry. Who was he to accuse her of being a coward? But, after a moment, she realized he was right. She was afraid.

"And rightly so," he continued. "I was always afraid before going into battle."

"You!" said Emma, in surprise. "But I've read about you! You were one of the most courageous and successful knights of your time. You're a legend!"

"I might have been successful, but courage is always a struggle. It's only the weak-minded who don't feel any fear."

Emma looked at Horatio with new eyes. "But how did you

go into battle if you were afraid?"

"Ahh," said Horatio, "it wasn't always easy. I knew I was fighting for a just cause. I was protecting others and battling evil. That helped me to overcome some of my fears. But not all of them. I think there was always a little fear. But that's normal."

Emma nodded slowly, feeling slightly better.

"And, even more importantly," said Horatio, "I always tried to believe in myself, no matter what. Win or lose, all I could do was the best I had in me."

Emma looked at Horatio. "Do you believe in me?" she asked, haltingly.

"Of course," said Horatio, with a smile. "It would be impossible not to. You're incredible. But you need to believe in yourself."

"I'm not sure I do," said Emma slowly. "I'm not like the other girls here."

"No, you're not," said Horatio. "But that very difference is what makes you incredible. And it's what makes you who you are. Use those differences. They will give you strength."

"But what if I can't do it?" said Emma, fearfully. "What if I make the wrong choice?"

"We can't know the future," said Horatio. "But I know you'll do the best you can. You are truly special. And you're very powerful. Use your gifts, be true to yourself, and you will succeed."

Emma looked at Horatio gratefully. "I don't know what I would do without you. But I suppose I should try to get some sleep now."

"Sleep would do you good," replied Horatio. "You're going to need all of your energy tomorrow."

Emma nodded and began to make her way to the library door.

"You better hurry back," said Horatio. "I'll be very lonely without your visits!"

"Don't worry," said Emma, trying her best to sound

confident. "I'll be back before you know it!"

Chapter 14
The Place Between

It was very early the next morning. All of the gray witches were assembled in the Great Hall. There was a hushed expectancy about the group, broken only by earnest whispers every now and then.

Emma and Ms. Stanwick were standing slightly apart from the crowd.

"You know what you have to do?" asked Ms. Stanwick, looking earnestly into Emma's face.

"Yes," answered Emma quietly. She was still scared but resolute. She knew she had a job to do.

"You'll be okay," said Ms. Stanwick. "I know you can do this."

Emma felt the tears almost start to her eyes. This was not what she had expected from Ms. Stanwick.

"Thank you," she whispered, "that means more to me than you know."

Ms. Stanwick smiled slightly, and then turned to face the assembly.

"In a few moments, we are going to depart," she began in a grave voice. "It's been a long time since we've had to enter the Place Between. I know some of you have never experienced this realm at all. It's unlike anything that you've ever known. It will feel like you're in a dream or a dense fog. But please don't be deluded. Everything that you will see, hear, and experience is very real."

"All of us," she said, gesturing to include all of the assembled gray witches, "will be fighting against the Red

Witches' army. While we are keeping her army occupied, Emma will make her way to the Stone Tower and destroy the Red Plague. As soon as Emma completes her task, I will transport us all back to this room."

Everyone in the room nodded grimly, aware of the difficulty of the mission they were undertaking.

Ms. Stanwick turned and raised her hands, ready to begin her transportation spell.

However, before she could begin, she paused, as if noticing something for the first time.

Cora, wearing an opalescent, shimmering blue-green sash was standing next to Emma.

Ms. Stanwick opened her mouth to say something, and then gazed more closely at Cora.

"Of course," she murmured. "An Earth Witch! How could I have been so blind!"

Emma smiled and grasped Cora's hand. Cora, who looked slightly pale, tried to smile back at her.

"We'll be okay," whispered Emma, "we'll get through it together."

Before Cora could respond there was a rush of wind and the room went dark. The transportation spell had begun.

*****

For several moments, all Emma could hear was a horrible rushing wind. Everything that was familiar had disappeared and she was immersed in a gray liquid sea, murky and strange. Gradually, the fog began to lift and Emma could begin to make out objects. But she wasn't at Witches Academy anymore.

She was in the courtyard of a large fortress, or at least what looked like a fortress. It was hard to tell for sure because there was a strange haze obscuring everything around her. Just as Ms. Stanwick had said, it felt as if she was in a dream world.

Emma looked around, and suddenly realized that she wasn't alone. Cora, and all of the other grey witches were also

116

spread out around the courtyard, all looking a bit dazed.

Before Emma could do or say anything, she was hit with the first onslaught. She felt herself fall to the ground, almost blinded by a flash of light that came from across the courtyard. As Emma tried to get up she looked ahead of her and fear froze her in place. There, before her eyes, was the Red Witch's Army.

The army was horrifying. Emma had never seen anything like it before. Hundreds of women, pale white, with dead, unseeing eyes, dressed all in blood red robes, were rushing towards them.

"Quick!" said a voice above her. "Get up before they reach us!"

Emma felt a hand pulling her up and then saw Cora standing over her.

"We need to get to the Stone Tower before it's too late," said Cora.

Emma nodded her head and shook herself. She still felt muddle headed. This place had a strange power that was making it difficult for her to focus.

"I feel it too," said Cora, "but I think it should wear off soon."

Cora grabbed Emma's hand and the two girls began to make their way towards the largest tower of the fortress, the Stone Tower. The tower was constructed of smooth black marble, and, even from a distance, it looked scary and forbidding. It was on the far side of the courtyard, a long way for the two girls to traverse in open sight of the Red Witch's army.

As they began, Emma could hear Ms. Stanwick organizing the grey witches to do battle against the horrible enemy before them.

"Let's hope that they can keep them busy while we get to the tower," said Emma, with a shudder.

Emma and Cora ran as fast as they could across the courtyard. Emma glanced back a few times at the battle raging behind them. It seemed as if the grey witches were keeping the army at bay. None of the Red Witch's army had broken off in pursuit of them.

"I think we're going to make it..." began Emma. Suddenly her voice died in her throat. Standing before them was a member of the Red Witch's army, blocking their path.

"You didn't think it would be this easy, did you?" asked the woman, in a strange, hissing voice.

The two girls were both frozen in place by terror. All of the spells Emma might have used against the woman were gone from her head.

Emma watched, paralyzed, as the woman raised her hands above her head. She was going to destroy them. And there was nothing Emma could do.

Suddenly, there was a huge crash and a flash of light, and, to Emma's shock, the woman fell to the ground before them. What had happened?

"Got her!" said a voice behind them.

Emma and Cora whirled about in surprise. There, grinning at them, was Esmerelda.

"It turns out explosions do come in handy every so often," she said, her grin widening.

"Thank you," breathed Emma, in relief. "You saved us!"

"You're welcome," said Esmerelda. "But you should go, now!"

Emma nodded, took Cora by the arm, and the two began running again.

*****

After what seemed like an eternity, the two girls stood in front of the Stone Tower.

Emma's heart sank as she looked at it. It was a deep, shiny black, darker than anything she had ever seen before. It seemed to emanate a bone chilling cold, and Emma shuddered as she stood gazing before her.

"This is where we part ways," said Emma finally, trying to sound braver than she felt.

Cora squeezed Emma's hand tightly. "I know," she said, softly. "I'll wait for you and keep watch."

Emma started towards the small doorway at the base of the tower. However, just as she was about to enter the door, a strange noise echoed throughout the courtyard. Suddenly, a thick, thorn covered vine broke its way out of the earth and began to entwine itself around the tower, completely blocking her entry in just a few moments.

"Don't worry," said Cora. "You said you were going to need my help."

Cora closed her eyes, raised her arms, and then moved them slowly towards the thorns.

As Emma watched, the vine stopped growing and large parts of it began to wither and die. In a moment, the doorway was accessible again, with a space just large enough for Emma to pass through.

Emma glanced at Cora, who was pale and shaking.

"Go...quickly!" she whispered. "I'll hold them off for as long as I can."

Emma ran towards the tower door, squeezed herself through the small opening, and quickly ascended the winding stone staircase.

At the top of the stairs, there was another door that led into a small room. Before she could stop and think about what lay beyond, Emma burst into the room. To her surprise, all she saw in the room was an elegant desk with a tall, serene woman seated calmly behind it. Was this the dreaded Red Witch?

The woman looked up and smiled at Emma. She gestured towards a chair in front of the desk.

"You must be Emma. I've been expecting you" she almost purred, in a soft sweet voice. "Why don't you sit down?"

Emma was taken aback. This woman, although dressed in a dark red robe, didn't look evil. She actually seemed nice. She was very tall and thin. Her face was extremely pale with lovely, delicate features. Her golden hair was pulled back and twisted atop gracefully her head.

Emma wasn't sure what to do, but she certainly wasn't about to sit down. She couldn't let her guard down.

"Ahh," said the Red Witch, as she watched Emma hesitate. "You don't trust me. I can only imagine what you've heard about me."

Emma swallowed hard. She wasn't going to be tricked by this woman.

"I'm here to stop you," said Emma.

"Of course you are," replied the Red Witch, gently. "I know all about you. You're on a little Quest, or whatever it is that they call it these days. I think I was on a Quest of my own at one point...oh so long ago. But I learned quickly that there is so much more to being a witch than what those silly gray witches teach."

"Where is it?" said Emma, trying not to listen to what the Red Witch was saying. Her voice was seductive. It seemed to draw Emma in, despite her resistance.

"Right there, ready for you," said the Red Witch, nodding towards a cell phone that was sitting on the table in front of her. "The entire program for the Red Plague is stored in that phone."

Emma looked a bit confused. Was it going to be this easy?

"Ahh, you're surprised," said the Red Witch, smiling slightly at Emma's confusion. "But there's nothing to be surprised about. I know what you're here for."

Emma walked closer to the table, expecting a trap of some sort.

She could see the phone clearly. The screen was transparent and there were several buttons clearly visible.

"It's just as they told you," said the Red Witch. "Just press the blue button and the entire disease will be destroyed. It's as easy as that."

Emma came closer to the table. The phone was within her reach. She was about to pick it up when the Red Witch continued speaking.

"But, if you press the other button, the red one, it will be better for you in the long run..."

Emma paused, trying not to be interested by what the Red Witch was saying. She didn't need to know about the red button. All she had to do was stop the plague, and that was within her reach already.

Before she could stop herself, Emma felt herself asking, "Why? What does the red button do?"

"I was hoping you would ask," purred the Red Witch as she got up from her place behind the desk.

She stood before Emma, tall and graceful, almost regal in her bearing.

"The red button will change everything for you. You will gain power and mastery! The power that you've wanted all of your life, that's never been within your grasp, it's all right there!"

"How do you know what I want?" said Emma, with trepidation.

"Emma, don't you know by now that one like mind recognizes another?" said the Red Witch softly. "I know you because you're just like me. You've been mistreated your whole life. No one has ever helped you or realized your true worth. Until now...."

"I'm not like you," Emma protested weakly

"Maybe," replied the Red Witch. "Perhaps that's what you think now. But if I were to offer you the power of which I speak, I think the choice would be easy for you. Think of all of the people who've ever hurt you....the instructors at your former school, all of those girls that snubbed you and persecuted you, the petty humiliations that you've had to endure your entire life...wouldn't revenge be so sweet? It would be in your grasp...you could do whatever you wanted...you would be completely in control for the first time in your life..."

Emma's head still felt fuzzy. She was trying to fight against what the Red Witch was saying, but she could feel a response in her heart. The dark part of her did want revenge. She had suffered and she wanted retribution. That wasn't necessarily bad, was it? She should have the power to punish those who hurt her.

"Ahh," said the Red Witch, a small smile forming over her lovely face. "I see you know what I'm talking about. You're perfectly right, you know. There's nothing wrong in meting out punishment, especially to those who have hurt you...."

"I can't," said Emma in a shaky voice. She willed herself to reach for the phone and press the blue button, but she couldn't. She was mesmerized by the Red Witch.

"And then of course," continued the Red Witch, "there are your so-called friends. I don't know if I'd even call them friends. If you think about it, what have they ever done to help you? What they're really interested in is your power! That's why they sent you here to stop me. They're using you because you're so much more powerful than they are. Look how pathetic and powerless they look right now!"

The Red Witch waved her hand and Emma could see, quite clearly, the battle that was going on below. Her friends were losing. The grey witches were falling, some not getting up again.

"Unless you have power," said the Red Witch, "everyone suffers...right or wrong. But with power, you get to control everything. You get to decide who suffers and who doesn't! Join me Emma, and help me make the world right."

The Red Witch waved her arm again and the raging battle disappeared.

Emma was lost. She felt paralyzed. The allure of what the Red Witch had offered her was overpowering. She could finally make things right on her own terms, without all of the difficulties that seemed to beset the grey witches and their way of thinking. Look at them! They were losing! It they were so right, why didn't they win?

"I've offered this power to others before," said the Red Witch. "You saw them in the army outside, hollow shells of

122

women. They couldn't handle the power that I hold. But Emma, you're different. You're the first one that could truly wield this power without having it overwhelm you. Together, we'll be able to do anything!"

Emma felt that the Red Witch was right. Hadn't she known from the very first that she was destined to be the most incredible witch of all time?

Emma felt herself yielding, and there was nothing she could do. She had nothing she could hold onto to save herself. She reached into her pocket desperately, her hand groping for the Black Knot that Cora's Aunt Ethel had given her. She'd decided to bring it with her at the last minute, but she hadn't planned on using it. Somehow dark magic seemed just as bad as yielding to the Red Witch. She knew it wasn't the right path. But she didn't have a choice.

As Emma searched in her pocket, something cold and metallic jabbed into her hand. What was it? Her hand closed around the object. Suddenly she knew. It was the necklace that Lindsay had given her months ago when she had left Williamson. But how had it gotten into her pocket? She was certain she hadn't put it there herself.

Emma grasped the necklace tightly. As she did so, she thought of Lindsay and Cora and Horatio, Thora and Nedra, Ms. Harfield and Ms. Stanwick, and all of the girls at Witches' Academy. They had all been strangers to her just a short time ago, but they had offered her something she'd never received from anyone before.

As Emma thought about all of her friends, she felt her own power for good surging. The lure of the Red Witch's dark power paled in comparison to the power she knew she had within her.

"What about love?" said Emma, looking directly at the Red Witch.

"Love!" said the Red Witch, almost in snarl. It was the first time that Emma had heard anything approaching ugliness come out of her mouth.

She quickly regained her composure and tried to smile. "Love is for weaklings and fools," she said. "How many times have you been treated with love? It doesn't exist."

"No," said Emma, with a surge of pride. "You're wrong. Love does exist."

Emma paused for a moment and looked at the Red Witch with new eyes. Suddenly, the woman before her looked weak and ugly.

"I don't need your power," Emma continued. "I have my own. And I'm going to use it to stop you."

As Emma said this, the sweet smile that had graced the Red Witch's face since the beginning of their interview turned hard and brittle.

"You've made the wrong choice," she snapped. As she spoke her face transformed with anger. Her eyes glowed red and her lips took on the color of blood.

Emma walked calmly towards the desk where the phone carrying the Red Plague was sitting. She reached for the phone, hoping she could get to it before the Red Witch. But it was too late. The Red Witch knocked the phone off the table before Emma could reach it.

"You're not going to beat me!" she screamed, her anger and rage overwhelming her.

Emma paused and then raised her hands above her head.

"Yes I am," she said, in a slow, even voice.

Emma closed her eyes and focused all her strength on casting her spell. There was one spell that they hadn't learned in school. But she knew what it was now. And it was going to be the easiest spell she had ever cast, the Eleventh Spell, the spell of pure love.

After what seemed like a very long time, Emma lowered her hands. The Red Witch had sunk to her knees before her. One more spell would end everything. But Emma knew she couldn't do it. Her spells were for love, not hatred or vengeance.

"Do it!" hissed the broken figure before Emma. "What are

you waiting for?"

"I can't," said Emma. "I don't want to destroy."

As Emma said this, the Red Witch gave an ear piercing shriek. Emma watched in horror as the woman disintegrated into nothingness, leaving behind a pile of red dust. What had just happened?

With difficulty, Emma dragged her attention away from the horrific spectacle. She needed to hurry if she was going to save her friends. She looked around to locate the crucial cell phone. It was lying on the floor, underneath the desk. She grabbed the phone and jammed her finger onto the blue button. Then, she ran towards the stairs leading out of the tower.

"Please don't let me be too late," she whispered, as she ran.

Chapter 15
Resolution

Emma tried to scream but nothing came out. She was running as fast as she could, trying to get away from an army of Red Witches. She knew that there was something very important that she had to do, but she couldn't remember what it was. And she was running out of time...

Emma awoke with a start. Her eyes fluttered open and she sat up in bed abruptly. Where was she? What had happened?

In a moment, remembrance came flooding back. The Red Witch, the plague, the Place Between...it had all happened. But how had she gotten here, back into her own room at the academy? And what had happened to everyone else? Had she been too late? Had the plague been unleashed?

Emma looked around and tried to get out of bed, but, as she started to stand up, her legs buckled underneath her.

"Oh no you don't," said Thora, who had just bustled into her room. "You're still a bit too weak for that."

"What happened?" asked Emma, rubbing her head in confusion. "How did I get back here? And what's wrong with me?"

"Nothing's wrong with you, thank goodness!" said Thora, with a smile. "But battling a Red Witch will take it out of you. You'll be yourself again in a few more days. But for now, you must rest."

"How long have I been sleeping?" asked Emma.

"About two days," replied Thora. "But that's normal. Your body and mind are exhausted. You expended a lot of power to defeat the Red Witch."

"But is everything okay?" asked Emma, with concern. "I wasn't too late?"

"No," said Thora, gently. "Of course you weren't. We knew you could do it. Everyone is very proud of you."

"Did all of the gray witches make it back safely?" asked Emma.

Thora nodded. "Yes," she replied. "Thanks to you. After you defeated the Red Witch, you gathered us all up and cast the spell to get us back here. We have some injuries, but that's to be expected..."

As Thora trailed off, Emma looked at her more closely. There was something about her face that she didn't like. She could tell that Thora was holding something back.

"What aren't you telling me?" said Emma, suspiciously. "There's something else going on."

Thora hesitated and then began speaking in a gentle voice. "I knew you would see through me. We didn't want to tell you right away...not until you were better..."

"What?" demanded Emma. "Tell me what?"

"It's about Cora...." began Thora.

"Oh no," said Emma. Her mind flashed back to when she had last seen Cora, outside the Red Witch's tower, desperately battling the thorn covered vines.

"Is she...." Emma began, hardly trusting her voice to say the words.

"She's still alive," said Thora, softly. "But it's not certain that she's going to recover. She was badly hurt during her fight against the Red Witch's thorns. It's a wonder she was able to hold them off as long as she did..."

"I have to see her," said Emma. "I don't care about resting! Where is she?"

"She's down the hall, in one of the instructor's rooms. We thought she would be more comfortable there. But you really shouldn't go now. You need to rest yourself. And there's nothing you can do."

"I know," said Emma, a lump in her throat. "But I need to

see her."

*****

A few moments later, Emma and Thora were outside the door to Cora's room. To her surprise, she saw Gavin stationed at the door.

"He hasn't left since we brought her here," whispered Thora to Emma.

"Only a few moments," said Thora, "I want you back in bed as soon as you've seen her."

Emma looked at Gavin. His entire demeanor was changed. Gone was the arrogant swagger and self-assured vanity. Instead, his face was pale and his eyes looked desperate.

Gavin nodded at Emma. He looked as if he was too tired to speak.

"You've been here the whole time," said Emma, looking at Gavin with newfound respect.

"Yes," he said softly. "I'm waiting...to talk to her. I know she's going to get better. She has too," he said fiercely.

Emma took his hand and squeezed it hard. "She will," she answered with determination.

"Her aunt is in there with her right now," said Gavin.

Emma felt a moment of surprise. Aunt Ethel, a Black Witch, at Witches' Academy?

Emma opened the door softly and entered the room.

She could see Cora's aunt sitting absolutely still over the bed. Emma walked towards her quietly.

"I'm glad you've come," said the Aunt Ethel softly, without turning around. "I've been waiting for you."

Emma came up next to the bed and looked down at Cora. If possible, she was even more lovely than Emma had ever seen her. But she was dreadfully pale and her face clearly showed that she was in pain.

"She's suffering," said Emma.

"Yes," replied Ethel. "She's fighting a very difficult battle."

"I wish there was something I could do..." said Emma, falteringly.

"There is," said Aunt Ethel. "How strong do you feel?"

Strong enough to do anything to help Cora," said Emma.

"Then take my hand," said Ethel. "We're going to bring her back."

*****

A few weeks later, Emma was sitting in the library with Horatio. She couldn't believe everything that had happened in such a short space of time.

"It looks good on you," said Horatio, admiring Emma's silver sash. "I think silver is your color. It's much better than gray. And you're the only one! You are definitely the most incredible witch of all time, as I keep saying."

Emma smiled at him. "I only have it because of you," she said gratefully. "The Eleventh Spell and believing in myself, love and friendship...you helped me realize what all those things are."

"Whatever do you mean?" said Horatio, his translucent skin reddening slightly.

"What you told me before I fought the Red Witch...it saved me," she replied.

"You would have been fine without my help," said Horatio, modestly.

"I don't know," said Emma, uncertainly. "The Red Witch was very strong."

"But you were stronger," said Horatio. "Or you wouldn't be here now."

"Yes," said Emma, "but you helped me. No matter what you say to the contrary!"

Horatio smiled. "I'm glad to have helped," he said. "But I don't think you can give me all of the credit. You're an amazing witch Emma! The best I've ever come across."

Emma looked at him and returned his smile, but a bit

sadly. "And to thank you for your help, I have a gift for you."

"A gift?" said Horatio in surprise. "Whatever could you have for me? There's nothing I want, unless it's..." he trailed off, his voice expressing surprise, doubt, and yearning.

"You don't think I became a Siler Witch without learning a few tricks! I know how to send you back," said Emma.

Horatio flew up from where he was hovering at the table and somersaulted around the room. "You can't be serious!" he said with elation. "But I know you wouldn't say something like that unless you were certain!"

"Of course I'm certain," said Emma. "But part of me doesn't want to send you back," she added. "I'll miss you."

Horatio came down from ceiling level where he had catapulted himself. He looked at her with kindness. "I know," he said. "You're the one person I will miss. I wish I could bring you with me. But I suspect that it won't be forever. I feel as if we're going to meet again."

Emma smiled at him. "I hope you're right," she replied. "This old library won't be the same without you. What are the witches going to complain about?"

*****

Emma sat down heavily in Ms. Stanwick's office. She had been through so much already. She didn't know if she could handle anything else. But she was now a Silver witch...the only one in the world! And, as such, she was getting her first assignment. She knew that she didn't want to leave the academy. There was so much for her there. It was the first place she'd felt at home, the first place she'd had real friends, friends who were like family.

"I hope you know how proud of you everyone is at the academy," said Ms. Stanwick, smiling at Emma. "What you did to defeat the Red Witch was amazing. We would have lost without you."

"It wasn't just me," said Emma. "Everyone was needed to

defeat the Red Witch."

Ms. Stanwick, looking at Emma with affection. "You've come a long way since you first arrived here," she said "You've undergone trials that most witches will never undergo. And you had to face two tests when you fought the Red Witch, not just one."

Emma looked at her curiously. "What do you mean?"

"You had to choose between good and evil, the gray witches and all that we stand for and the dark power that the Red Witch offered you. That was the first test. But you also had to choose between mercy and vengeance. You could have destroyed the Red Witch. But you didn't."

"It was tempting at first," said Emma honestly. "But I couldn't do it."

"The good won out in you," smiled Ms. Stanwick. "And once that happens, there is no more danger from the dark."

Emma nodded. She knew what Ms. Stanwick way saying was true.

"So that is why we're offering you a teaching position here at the school," continued Ms. Stanwick. "We want you to instruct the new witches. I think at this point you're more than qualified. There's so much you have to offer. Of course, we'll want to do a little training before you start. But that's normal procedure for all of our new instructors."

Emma was flabbergasted. This was not what she had expected!

"Wait a minute," she said, trying to control her excitement. "I can stay? You aren't sending me away?"

"Of course not," said Ms. Stanwick. "You're much too valuable to us. And, what with all of the publicity we've gotten since we destroyed the Red Plague, we need as many instructors as we can get. Applications are coming in by the thousands! Ms. Harfield alone has about 20 students she's sending to us already, including a few girls you know, someone named Lindsay, I think she said. We may need to build a new wing...."

Emma almost ran out of the Ms. Stanwick's office. Cora was waiting for her in the hallway.

"Well," she said eagerly. "What did she say?"

Emma took a deep breath before she exploded with her news. She was still a bit taken aback anytime she saw Cora. Cora was getting better everyday. She was going to make a fully recovery. It was almost unbelievable! But she still looked so weak and fragile. Emma didn't want to do anything to injure her.

She took another deep breath and then began speaking. "They want me to stay," she said, trying hard to contain the excitement in her voice. "They need instructors...and I'm going to be one!"

Cora beamed. "That's wonderful news!" she said. "That means we're going to be here together. Thora and Nedra said they need me here too, to help with all of the new students!"

Emma beamed at her friend. It all seemed almost too good to be true!

"Now come on," said Cora, as she took Emma by the hand and led her down the hallway. "I promised Gavin and Winthrop we'd meet them this afternoon and we're already late. I have an outfit that will be perfect for you already picked out."

Emma groaned, but allowed herself to be led away by Cora. She felt truly happy for the first time in her life. She finally belonged somewhere.

THE END?

STARGAZER
BOOKS

Stargazer Books is a small publishing house with big dreams . . . to find out more please visit

www.stargazerbooks.com

If you enjoyed this book and would like to help us "spread the words" . . . please leave a review on

or LIKE and SHARE on

Look for other books by author Kerry Marie Sloan

https://amzn.to/2wtoxod

The Fountain of Death
(A Perfectly Silly Mystery)

Young Adult Fiction
for ages 11 and up

The Book of Westmere
First in The Guardian Series

Young Adult Fiction
for ages 11 and up

ATNAS
The South Pole Elf

Children's Book
Please read to your child

We hope you enjoy books by author Kerry Marie Sloan

Witches Academy

The Guardian Series by author Kerry Marie Sloan

The Book of Westmere
The Four Towers